VICIOUS REVENGE

A REVERSE HAREM MAFIA ROMANCE

BEAUTY & THE BRATVA

MIKA LANE

HEADLANDS PUBLISHING

COPYRIGHT

Headlands Publishing
4200 Park Blvd. #244
Oakland, CA 94602
USA

BE THE FIRST TO KNOW...

Want more heat, heart,
and bad boys who know what they're doing?
Join my list and I'll send the steam straight to your inbox,
starting with a deliciously naughty story:

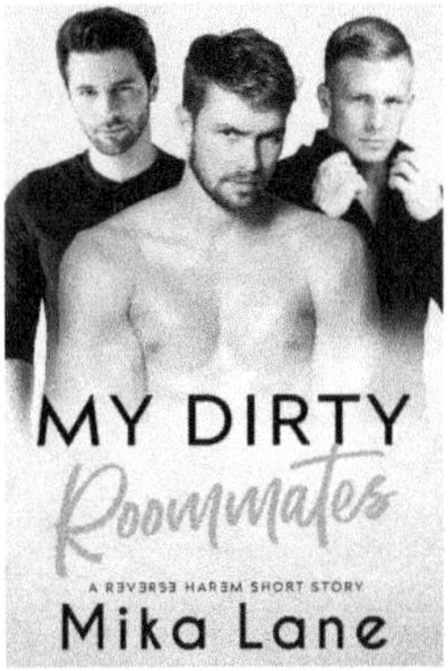

SIGN UP TO MY MAILING LIST!

Or visit:

https://geni.us/free-book-signup

PROLOGUE

Charleigh

I'm still bruised and battered, thanks to the fucker Dimitri, so I lean carefully against the elevator wall with my good arm as we descend. Kir leans toward me to hear the words I'm mumbling, but even I'm not sure what I'm saying.

Whatever it is, I'm making it up on the spot.

I have to. It's a prayer, and I don't know any prayers.

Kir knows this. He's been where I am right now. When he had his accident with Clara all those years ago, he probably did the same thing.

It didn't help him. It may not help me.

And I know that right now, Kir wants nothing more in the world than for my prayers to be answered.

If the explosion that has undoubtedly taken Stacey's life also grabbed my sister's, that'll be the end of me. There's no way, absolutely no fucking way, I will survive. If I don't die of a broken heart, I'll be no more than a shell of my former self. A waste of flesh, just taking up room on this earth.

A useless piece of shit, that's what I'll be.

Which means I'll essentially be gone to Kir and his brothers. Oh, they'll take care of me, no doubt. They always will. That, I know. But I won't be their girl, their partner, their lover.

Not the way they would want me to be, anyway.

When the elevator opens to the ground floor, I bolt. Dominika said the accident was a few blocks from the club, and it's clear the direction I need to go in because there's black smoke billowing into the sky and the sound of fire engines getting closer.

But before I break into a sprint, Kir grabs my arm and turns to the front door security guy, who stands guard like he always does, but whose lips are right now drawn into a thin, rigid line as he watches the smoke several blocks away. He has his hand on his gun holster as he should, ready for any other bullshit that might come our way.

"Call for backup," Kir yells at him. "Niko's car exploded. It may have been a bomb. Get everybody. Now!"

I shake off Kir while he's still barking orders at security and start running, faster than I thought I could, considering I have one arm in a sling and am wearing high-heeled boots. But if the person you loved more than anyone in the world was in danger, you would do the same.

Kir's catching up, but I'm damn fast. He finally gains on me and as we round a corner in the direction of the accident, I stumble, crashing to one knee. Before me is the burning hulk of what used to be Niko's Audi, T-boned by a giant big rig truck.

The Audi I've been driving, and in fact drove just this morning with my sister as passenger.

The knee I fall on kills but only for a moment, then strangely stops altogether, I guess because of some adrenaline thing, even though I see blood through the torn hole in my jeans. Pushing back to my feet with my good arm, I continue to run, screaming incoherently for Evie, and getting closer to the fire. Too close.

A cop grabs me. I try to wrestle out of his hold, screaming 'my sister.' But instead of releasing me, he doubles down, lifting me up by the waist, effectively immobilizing me. I kick and twist as if I might be able to get free. I can't.

"Officer, I'm with her," Kir says when he catches

up. He seizes hold of the hair on the back of my head "Goddammit, Charleigh, stop," he yells.

The cop's eyes widen when he sees Kir's rough treatment, but when I go limp, like a kitten picked up by her scruff, he lets me go. I crumble to the ground, screaming and sobbing.

"Officer, how many people in the car? How many?" Kir yells over the noise of all the chaos.

"One, we're pretty sure. Why? Do you think there were more?"

Kir nods as I wail. I can't stop myself.

"We're looking for a teenager who might have been in the car. Have you seen a teenager?" he asks.

The cop stands and surveys the crazy scene. "Sir, there's one over there, on the curb, talking to two other officers."

I turn to look, hoping against hope. The sledgehammer driving into my chest lifts, and for a moment I can breathe, think, and see again. My sister, that little shit who is going to be the end of me, is sitting with her head in her hands, being questioned by two cops.

I scream her name with more force than a violent volcano could muster, and almost everyone at the accident scene hears me, but when the most important one of all does, she starts running for me.

CHAPTER ONE

Kir

Evie looks up at the sound of her name and when she spots us, her face horrified at the vision of her sister in hysterics, the cops step aside and let her run to us.

She collapses into Charleigh's arms, just about matching her sister's wailing.

"Oh my god," Charleigh screams, "I thought you might be… I thought you were in the car."

"I'm sorry, Charleigh, I'm so sorry," Evie cries. "I've put you through so much. I promise to stop, I promise to behave. Please forgive me," she begs.

I get to my feet. We're now surrounded by three officers who want to know what the hell is going on.

But first things first.

I step closer to the two men and one woman in

uniform and lower my voice. "Are there… is there any chance of… survivors?"

I choke on this last word, so close to the conversation I had when I lost Clara in the accident, words I never thought I'd have to utter again.

The female cop grimaces and shakes her head sadly. "Sorry, sir, I'm afraid not. Do you know the person who was driving? Was she a… friend?"

Ugh. Papa always taught us to share as little as possible with the police. Every little bit of information leads to more and more questions.

So I tread carefully. "That's my brother's car. We loaned it to one of our employees who was picking up her little boy at school."

One of the other cops takes notes. "What did you say her name is, sir? The victim?"

"Um, Stacey. Her name is Stacey. It *was* Stacey," I say, the flames now under control thanks to the fire department's water hoses.

"Stacey *what,* sir?" he asks.

Shit. I have no idea of her last name.

"Uh, I'm not sure, Officer. I mean, I'm kind of rattled right now, and her last name isn't coming to me. I'm sorry," I lie.

Charleigh looks up from her sister huddle and glares at me. She knows I'm full of shit. "Jones. Her last name is Jones," she calls.

"Right," I add. "Jones." Like I actually knew all along.

Jesus Christ. One of our employees just died and I have no freaking idea what her last name was. What a douche I am.

"Do we know how it happened?" I ask, hoping to redirect the conversation.

They gesture toward an older gentleman who pulls off his trucker hat and runs his fingers through his thinning grey hair. He's talking to another cop.

He looks oddly familiar.

Do I know a truck driver?

The officers and I approach him and the other officer questioning him.

"She ran a light. Officer, she ran the light," he insists.

His rig is mostly fine, and he's completely without injury himself, but his hands shake violently, and he keeps looking down, avoiding everyone's gaze.

I watch quietly as he answers questions with brief *yes's* and *no's*.

Interesting. He's not avoiding everyone's gaze. He's avoiding *mine,* I find, as he makes eye contact with the cops.

What the fuck is going on here?

The hairs on the back of my neck stand at attention, and I discreetly pat the side where my firearm is holstered. The last thing I want to do is alert the cops that I'm carrying, but when my instincts tell me something isn't right, I can't help but check.

"Okay, we get that she went through the light, Mr. Michaels, but I don't think that would cause such an explosion. Are you sure you didn't see anything else?"

The officer's right to ask. A car doesn't explode like that without some sort of help.

"Nope. No, sir," he insists, glancing my way but looking back down before our eyes meet.

Something here…

No.

No fucking way. *No.*

Is this the man who…

I can't even think it.

I squeeze my eyes shut and wander back to the worst day of my life, one I have not willingly revisited in a long, long time.

When Clara and I crashed, we were T-boned by a big rig.

They hit her side of the car and killed her. I was injured but not badly. Not badly at all. But when they pulled me out of the car, there was a man, a truck driver, who kept insisting we'd run a red light…

Holy fuck. It's the same man.

What are the chances that the same guy driving a big rig T-bones one of the Alekseev cars several years later...

That's when my phone rings, startling me out of my reverie. I see Charleigh and her sister now sitting on the sidewalk curb, clutching each other. I grab the call, thinking it's one of our security guys.

"Yeah?" I snap.

I shouldn't take it out on them. This is beyond their control. And yet, if we can't avoid what I suspect was a simple car bomb, why are we spending so much on security? Someone's dead in spite of all our efforts, and that someone could have been any of us. Or Charleigh. And her sister.

For a moment, there is no sound but breathing on the phone and I figure it's a wrong number or fucking solicitation. But just as I start to hang up, someone finally speaks, slowly and deliberately. "I hear things are getting a little *hot* in your part of town, Kir. Sorry I didn't manage to *fire up* the right people."

Fucking Dimitri. He tops off his vile joke by cackling like the sick person he is.

I turn away from the crowd and lower my voice. The last thing I need is to give the cops any tips that would lead right back to me or my brothers.

"Dimitri, I have two words for you. *You're dead.*"

"Kir," he says, tsking his tongue. "That's not really two words. It's more like two and a half."

Oh that he were right in front of me at this moment. It would be his last, alive.

"I don't know where the fuck you are, but you know your days are numbered. You can't hide forever. And when we do find you, you'll know a slow, excruciating death, which is probably better than you deserve, but which my brothers and I will enjoy immensely."

"Challenge accepted, my childhood friend," he singsongs.

I should have beaten the fucker to death when I had the chance, back when I was ten years old and I could have lied and said he hit his head on the playground and *oh well.*

But that's okay. We're grown-ups now and finishing him off will be much more satisfying than it would have been twenty-plus years earlier.

CHAPTER TWO

Kir

"Come on," I say, helping Charleigh to her feet.

Evie takes her sister's other side and, avoiding her sore shoulder, steadies her. The adrenaline flood driving her earlier may have ceased, but she is still shaking.

"Where... where did the truck driver go?" she asks, craning her neck. "Isn't he responsible? Aren't they arresting him?"

"They took him to the station, sweetie. Are you sure you can walk? I can get someone to pick us up," I say.

Myself, I plan to get to the station as quickly as I can. I have some questions of my own for the man.

Charleigh shakes out her neck. "Let's walk. It will be good to catch our breath."

She's right, especially since I have some questions and want these two as my captive audience.

"Evie, what happened? How is it that Stacey was... in the car, and you were sitting there on the sidewalk?" I ask.

She looks afraid, but Charleigh pulls her close.

"Tell the truth, Evie. Tell Kir exactly what happened."

She looks nervous, as she should. She blew off her sister's instructions to stay put and went and left the club like the punk teenager that she is. Good thing she's not my sister. I'd be dragging her by the ear at this moment. Then I'd lock her in a room until she learned her lesson. But this is Charleigh's rodeo, and I have to let her run with it.

"I... well, Char told me I couldn't go with Stacey. I ran after her anyway when no one was around. The club is so boring and creepy with those men and that gross old lady. So, I was running to catch up at the red light. And then it happened," she says.

I stop walking, so they do too.

"Wait a minute. Stacey didn't run a red light? Then how did the truck hit her?" I ask.

Evie shakes her head *no*, and now looks more afraid than ever. "She was stopped at the light. I was catching up to her and she saw me in the rear-view mirror. She waved at me like she was going to wait, and the next second the truck plowed into her. Like he lost control or something. Right in front of me." She dissolves into sobs. "It was… so horrible."

Jesus Christ. It was intentional. I knew it when I recognized the driver. He lied about Stacey going through the light. What if my accident with Clara had been planned, as well? All these years, I thought it was plain rotten luck.

But if someone was out to kill me, they're now aiming for Niko? Or was it Charleigh who was the target?

The mood back at the club is solemn. We had Dominika ask the guests to leave for the day so we could make arrangements for our deceased employee. We locked the front doors for safety reasons and the security team checked every nook and cranny of our other cars. We also sent all staff at the compound back to their own cottages while sweeps were made of the main house as well as anyplace where a weapon or explosive device could be hidden.

This debacle caught us unaware. Completely. There could easily be others.

Charleigh and Evie are in one of the club bedrooms trying to relax, while my brothers and I pace Vadik's office.

Well, *I'm* pacing. Vadik is sitting at Papa's desk

looking like he might explode, and the more serene Niko has his eyes closed like he's meditating.

I knew he was into that shit, even though he denies it.

Weirdo.

"How in the fuck did this happen?" Vadik demands of no one in particular.

We're all wondering the same goddamn thing.

"This is what I think," I start, then take a pause before saying the heavy words I am about to. It's all too similar to what happened to Clara and me. And then there's that fucker of a truck driver. I'm heading to the station in a minute to get my hands on him. One call to a friend there, and they agreed to keep him until I arrived.

I continue. "The explosive was planted, who knows when. But it would only detonate when hit by the big rig. It wasn't a huge explosive, but big enough to kill the people in the front seat and start a fire to hide most if not all of the evidence," I explain. Then I told them about the call from Dimitri, taunting me, and really, all of us.

Niko's gaze snapped in my direction. "Holy fuck. Do you think..." He trails off.

"Yeah. I do, Niko," I say.

He doesn't need to finish. We're on the same page.

"So someone was watching the Audi and mistook Stacey for Charleigh?" he asks. It's more a statement than a question. We already know the answer.

Vadik nods. "They were watching and let the truck know where the car was headed. Easy target."

"He's dead. He's so fucking dead," I say of Dimitri.

"What do you think of sending Charleigh and Evie out of town for a while? To protect them?" Vadik suggests.

It's not a bad idea, although I feel better having them close. On one hand, it seems the best way to protect them, but on the other, keeping them here hasn't fared so well, given Charleigh's kidnapping, and now the car explosion.

I'm used to being in control of every situation around me, just like my brothers. Sure, we have rivals all over the place. But they rarely strike, much as they might like to. They know our return fire, so to speak, will be ten times what they initially sent our way. But these unrelenting hits are showing cracks in our systems. We have to be better. More vigilant.

It's been a fucking hard lesson to learn.

This is when I wish Papa were still here.

CHAPTER THREE

Charleigh

I never thought I'd say this, but it's good to be back in the club's dressing room with its rickety lockers, stained makeup table, and burned-out light bulbs. Dumpy as it may be, there's something comforting about it. I never would have expected positive feelings about this place, but when your life has been turned upside down so many times like mine has, so that you can no longer tell which side is up, the smallest bit of familiarity is a sanctuary. I am at peace here.

It's hard to say whether that's good or bad. On one hand, how pathetic that this is what represents the little good in my life right now. And on the other, at least I have someplace to go.

This is the place where I met Stacey, and we

became friends. We were in each other's lives for only a short period of time, but I'll never forget how kind she was to me when I first arrived. She made me believe I might just survive. The fact that I *did,* at least so far, I owe in great part to her. She showed me respect when no one else did. That made me feel human. It gave me hope.

I wish we could have been friends for years to come.

We don't appreciate what we have until it's gone. Life has taught me that more than once. I took for granted she'd be here at the club for the foreseeable future, and that I could always have a chat with her when I popped in. I wanted to hear about her little boy growing up, and her stories about making it even when the odds were stacked against her. She was amazing, making shit happen when others would have given up.

I open her locker, full of her things, untouched since the day of the car explosion.

I just spent the last two weeks holed up at the compound with my sister. The guys felt that, for the time being, it was the one place they could have absolute control over our safety. They quadrupled their security team and we could barely go to the bathroom without a guard following us. It seemed a little overkill to me, but if it made them feel better, I was happy to comply. After everything that happened, and considering I was still healing, I had no burning desire to do anything other than hunker down at home anyway, go on little walks with Evie, and explore the property.

Funny, I just called the compound *home*. I didn't see that one coming.

But what other home do I have at this point? Same with Evie. Our father wasn't capable of keeping her safe, just like he couldn't or wouldn't protect me, so this had to become her new home. Our new home.

This is probably not what our mother had in mind for us when she passed ten years ago, but under the circumstances, I want to believe she'd approve of how I've kept my sister with me, doing my best to keep her on the right track. I'm not always successful—in fact, I often am not. But at least I'm trying. That's more than anyone else is doing for the kid.

My arm is out of its sling, and while my shoulder is still sore, I'm able to reach the upper shelf of Stacey's locker. I asked the guys shortly after we lost her if they would leave her things alone, so I could go through them when I felt well enough. They were happy to oblige. It's not like anyone else was clamoring to go through what she left behind. Not even Dominika, who was more annoyed at having to find a new stripper than she was upset about the poor woman burning to death in a car explosion.

She's a gem, that one.

I go through a bag of makeup and remember how carefully Stacey would 'apply her face,' as she called it, every time she worked. She took such care with her appearance, saying that the better she looked, the better her tips were, and that she needed them for her boy.

Everything was for her boy.

The guys have said Stacey's mother and son would be looked after for the duration of their lives. I guess that means they're getting a whole pile of money, and I'm sure that will be a big help to them, on one level. But on the other, I'm sure they'd rather Stacey were still here.

I know that's what I'd prefer, given the choice.

After sorting through Stacey's makeup, trying to decide what to do with it, I pull her tote bag from the locker. In it, I find a couple women's magazines and a tattered copy of *Fifty Shades of Grey* that looks like she was carrying it around for quite some time. A page is dog eared about a quarter of the way in, so I guess she never got too far into it.

I pull the book to my chest and close my eyes,

hoping to feel her presence. And let her know how sorry I am she's gone. That it's my fault.

The guys don't know how long the explosive device was in the car, but it was just a matter of time before I drove it, and the big rig got me. They could have attacked me on my way to the club that morning, but instead waited for me to leave. Then they made the mistake of thinking I was driving when it was Stacey.

Who died instead of me. This ties my stomach into unrelenting knots every time I think about it, and doubly so since I'm now looking at the unremarkable remnants of her life. She didn't even see the truck coming, if she were indeed waving at Evie in the rearview mirror when she was hit.

The guys wouldn't tell me any more than that, except that the truck driver 'got what he had coming to him' as they said. And I don't really need to know more than that.

I slowly finger Stacey's belongings, showing them the respect she deserved but never got. I lay her things in neat piles on the makeup table and pull out the fake fur jacket she loved so much. I pull it on and twirl in front of the mirror. It smells like her and for a second I even look like her. I pop my hands in the pockets just like she used to when she came bouncing in, and I find a lipstick in one and what feels like money in the other. I pull it out and see it's the two hundred dollar bills I gave her.

This is when the lump in my throat is too much to bear. I sink into a cracked plastic chair and let big, fat tears run down my cheeks while I fold and unfold the money I'd meant to help her. I want to think it would have eventually been put to good use, and that she hadn't needed it just yet.

Another way life cheated this woman.

And then, the dressing room door flies open. It's Dominika.

Of course.

The last person I want to see at this moment.

"You're finally going through Stacey's crap, are you?" she huffs, propping her ass on the end of the makeup table like we're old girlfriends ready for a chat.

Since she's finally accepted I'm going to be around for a while, she's gotten nicer to me.

Somewhat.

She picks up a couple tubes of Stacey's lipstick and opens them to check their colors. I want to snatch them from her hands. She has no right to be touching Stacey's things. She was never kind to her, not for a moment. She didn't earn an entitlement to her memory. She was an affront to Stacey when she was alive. I won't let her be now that Stacey is... dead.

How I hate that word.

She tosses the lipstick back on the makeup table like they're trash. "You know, don't waste your time with this stuff. Just throw it all away."

Oh no. That was the wrong thing to say to me.

I rise to my feet, still wearing Stacey's fake fur coat. Dominika looks me up and down with amusement, like I'm a kid playing dress up.

C'mon, I am dying to say to her. *Make one more shitty remark. C'mon. Do it.* I stretch to my full height but am still dwarfed by Dominika thanks to her giant platform boots. It doesn't matter though, because my anger fills the room in a way I can't. As if she can sense that, she finally shuts her big mouth. For the most part.

She gets to her feet, gesturing at the things spread out over the table. "Suit yourself. There's nothing there of value," she scoffs.

"How would you know?" I say in a low, growly voice.

I surprise us both. But I don't care. It feels good to let loose some of my fury on this hideous excuse for a human being.

Unbothered, she shrugs me off. "Stacey didn't

have a pot to pee in. Of course, everything she left behind is junk," she sniffs

I take a step closer to Dominika, closer than I really want to be to her. "You wouldn't know if she had anything important, because you don't know what *is* important," I spit.

Her right eyebrow lifts and she chuckles at me with just as much disdain as she held for Stacey. "Okay. Okay, tough guy. Put me in my place, why don't you?" she taunts.

"Look, bitch," I say, inching closer. "I don't care if you're related to Niko. I don't care if you're related to the King of England. If you don't stay away from me with your nasty comments and ugly attitude, I will make sure you're as dead as Stacey."

Holy shit. I did it. I told the bitch off.

For a moment, her eyes grow wide. But she'll never let me get the better of her, so naturally has the last word. "Whatever. Whatever you say, Charleigh."

She saunters away like she's not bothered. But there's no way she missed the vitriol in my voice.

When she's gone, the room seems to refill with air and I take a deep breath. While I hope my standing up to her will keep her out of my hair for a while, I am also empowered. It feels good not to be afraid of her, to know I can call her out when I need to.

And I'm no longer afraid she'll find out I was the one who found her photos, the ones where she scratched out Mrs. Alekseev. In fact, I pull open her locker door. No big surprise, the box labelled *photos* is gone.

While I pack Stacey's things into grocery bags because that's all I could find, I wonder if her mother might like them. I remember how happy I was Victoria saved some of my mother's things for me.

As I finish, I see the corner of a photo wedged under the last locker in the row. I ease it out with a fingernail file and find it's one of the Alekseevs.

With their mother scratched out.

I tuck this into my pocket. I am sure it will come in handy, hopefully sooner rather than later.

CHAPTER FOUR

Charleigh

Something touches me in my sleep, jarring me awake. I haven't slept well since… Dimitri… and any sound or movement puts me on the defense. I ball my hand into a fist, ready to punch the throat of who or whatever touched me, when I realize it's Evie.

I fall back onto my pillow, horrified I nearly hit my sister. What the hell is wrong with me that I'm so on edge I'm ready to fight at any moment?

My self-defense classes are designed to give me the confidence to do my best, should I ever be faced with danger again. The instructors made it clear their objective is not to turn me into a one-woman killing machine, but to give me the basic skills to get out of trouble if I'm ever facing a dangerous situation again. The physical part is only one component, aside from awareness and verbal skills, but that's what has been occupying my thoughts around the clock.

Daydreaming about beating the shit out of someone is not what a person ought to have on their mind day and night, and yet the thought of tearing someone limb from limb is so… satisfying. It's like I've turned into an animal, that some sort of instinctual trigger switch has been turned on in me that I need to adjust.

If only I could figure out how.

I'm not supposed to come out of this an automatic punching machine. That's not how it works.

And yet here I am, my heart racing, grateful didn't punch out my sister like some kind of fighting machine, my sister whose foot simply brushed mine in bed.

Since my attack, and Evie coming to live in the compound, the poor kid wants to sleep with me every night, just like she did when our mother was murdered. She has her own room down the hall from mine, but damn if I can get her to spend any time there. As it is, she's either glued to me or in the kitchen with Gloria the housekeeper, who's been helping with her schoolwork, something we just got permission for her to do remotely.

She does need to go back to school eventually

and be around other kids her age, but the guys and I are still thinking through all the options. Do we want to send her to a private school? What will offer the most security and safety, since she's essentially now associated with the Alekseev clan? Or is it better for her to just remain on the compound and be homeschooled? How healthy would that be for a teenager? I'm not sure it's all that healthy for me, to be stuck here in this gilded cage.

I need to spend more time sorting this out, but I can't. All I can think about is hurting someone. Badly.

Niko says I have PTSD. He's probably right.

A sound comes from the other side of my bed. "Mmmm. Stop fidgeting. I'm trying to sleep," Evie mumbles.

If she slept in her own bed, my fidgeting wouldn't be a problem. But I don't go there. If this is one way I can comfort her, I'll suck it up.

I nudge her. "Time to get up anyway. You have schoolwork."

She groans and pulls the covers over her head. "Noooo," she whines. "I can do my schoolwork whenever."

I get up and head to my bathroom. "Get up and get ready *as if* you are going to school. You know we are keeping to a schedule, and that Gloria is downstairs waiting for you already."

She grumbles but climbs out of bed, her hair sticking in every direction, and heads to her own room, which she uses pretty much just for showering and changing her clothes.

In spite of her contrary nature, being here in the compound has been good for her. Her sassiness has decreased considerably, which, considering where we started might not be that big of an accomplishment, but it's something. And, I saw her in the guys' library the other day, picking out a couple books to read. Never thought I'd see that day.

Many of their books are special collector editions I assume should remain untouched, but no one—and I mean *no one*—is going to discourage Evie from reading a book. I don't care how priceless a volume it is, if she's interested in it, she has full access.

When it comes down to it, she's been a good distraction from my concerning one-track mind, where I'm coldly focused on turning myself into some sort of one-woman killing machine. The guys have noticed. Which is not a good thing.

A couple days ago, Niko suggested he and I practice sparring. While that's nice and all, sparring is not what protects you in an attack situation, I've learned. It's useless for street fighting. But I went along since he said it's good for endurance and strength building. It didn't bother my sore shoulder too much, not that he knows it still hurts. I keep that to myself.

Problem was, at the end of our practice, he leaned over to kiss me. And I punched him right in the chest.

When I did it, there was no thinking. It was as if my arm had a mind of its own, entirely independent from me, and *bam,* hit him like a well-honed reflex. Naturally, my small fist was no match for his muscular chest, and after his initial shock, he laughed it off.

But still. I was horrified.

So, it's good I'm learning this stuff. I just have to use it at the right time and place.

What worries me most is that I was glad I avoided the kiss, and that when I made contact with his chest, *it felt so good.* I only admitted this to myself later. I'm not proud of it, but when it comes down to it, I just don't want anyone touching me. For any reason. I pray that in time, these feelings will pass. I can't say for sure they will. But right now, I have no interest in being intimate. None.

Niko tells me I need to get out of my head or my training will falter. That could mean no revenge against Dimitri, which has pretty much become my sole reason for living. He told me that after my training sessions, he sees the life drain right out of my eyes, like the only way I feel alive is when I'm practicing, throwing punches, and thinking about hurting someone.

He may be right.

I am fueled by anger on my part, my sister's part, and Stacey's part. I'm overrun, polluted with rage, to the point I'm afraid it seeps out my pores with a noxious odor that will keep everyone I love away from me for the rest of my life. I am ugly on the inside like a rotten piece of fruit and can't find a single redeeming thing about myself except that I've sort-of gotten my sister on a new and better track for her life.

If that's all I manage to pull off right now, maybe that's enough. Maybe I should be thankful. I'm all about survival. I have to be. There's no room for the intimacy that soothed me before. There's no enjoying the special meals Chef has been making. It's like someone stole the heart right out of my chest and the tastebuds out of my mouth. I'm not happy about it. But it's my new reality.

I have little or nothing to say, having lost the art of conversation, and the scent of the flowers around me is sickening. I can't enjoy music, as I'm afflicted with a nonstop ringing in my ears. I can still see, thank God, but I feel like I'm looking down a long tunnel where revenge against Dimitri is at the end of it, very, very far away. Like so far away that I don't know I'll ever reach it, yet it's all I can think about, driven as I am by hatred—dark, ugly hatred that has pilfered my light. I know it and I know the guys know it.

I am trying to survive each day. It's not easy and there's room for nothing else. Will I get out of this abyss of misery and all-consuming anger?

Maybe. Maybe not.

CHAPTER FIVE

VADIK

"Guys, I don't mean to sound paranoid, but I've just put together some interesting facts, and I think we may have a bigger problem than we originally thought," Kir says.

Fuck all. As if there isn't already enough shit going down in our world. The attack on Charleigh and then the crash with Stacey has taken us away from all the other things we should be focused on. Sure, we have people working for us to keep things moving forward, but we can stay away for only so long. We need to get back to it, but dammit, with all this shit swirling around us, it's near impossible.

"What are you talking about?" I ask.

Kir paces the room, snapping the elastic band on his wrist that he normally uses on his too-long hair.

He takes a moment, like he's gathering his thoughts. "I haven't had the chance to tell you. The man who crashed into Stacey, the guy driving the big rig. Well, he looked familiar."

"He did?" I ask.

Kir rubs his hand over his face and looks vacantly around the room. "I'm... pretty sure he's the same truck driver who T-boned Clara and me a few years back."

No fucking way.

Impossible. Simply impossible. Too much of a coincidence.

Unless it's not.

Kir looks like he can hardly believe it himself, and yet, if I know my brother, he's checked his facts before making such an accusation.

"I did some digging. I had the guy grabbed when he was leaving the police station after giving his statement about Stacey's accident. Right now, he's being held at one of our facilities," he says.

"Are you serious? Are you really sure it's him?" Niko asks.

"Not one hundred percent, which is why he's still alive."

If this is true, if Kir is right, in spite of all these years believing his accident with Clara was just that —an accident, not deliberate or planned—how will he take it? Is he going to head back to that spiral of despair that almost killed him the first time around?

When Clara died, she took a big chunk of him with her.

We're quiet for a minute, digesting the implications.

"If that's what really happened, Kir, that both crashes were intentional, who do you think is behind it? Who do you think hired him?" I ask.

He presses his lips together. "Let's lay this out. What we do and don't know. Niko's car, being driven by Stacey, blew up when she was hit by the truck. We thought the truck was just incidental, but it seems like it was planned, used as a sort of detonator."

"Okay. Someone planted a bomb, and used a hired gun, a big rig driver, to fake an accident and make the thing explode," Niko says.

Kir is pacing so hard now he's making me dizzy, which is not good. This is the sort of shit that brings on my migraines. I close my eyes and listen.

"Right. The driver claimed Stacey went through a red light, but Evie was chasing the car, running after it, and saw it waiting at the light when the truck hit it. Stacey was never in the intersection, so the driver had to swerve toward her. He hit her so hard no one could tell whether she was in the intersection or not.

Evie insists Stacey never went through a light, red or otherwise. The truck just slammed into her, and then the driver lied about it. They hadn't counted on a witness like Evie. She saw the whole thing."

Holy fuck. "Can we get video of the intersection? Any cameras in the area?" I ask.

He shakes his head. "I've already checked that out. I suspect they chose that intersection *because* there are no cameras."

"So you're saying your accident with Clara" —I can't remember the last time I said the woman's name out loud— "played out the same? Some guy T-boned you, possibly on purpose? Was there a bomb in your car, do you think?"

I know this is hard for Kir to talk about. In fact, I'm surprised he is able to.

"I don't know. At the time, I never thought to look. The car was towed to the wrecking yard. I never saw it again. But if there had been one, it failed to detonate. The truck crashing into us accomplished the one thing it was probably never meant to —killing Clara instead of me."

I open my eyes again to see he's taken a seat and is holding his head in his hands. Poor bastard.

"Okay. So who's behind it?" I ask.

"That's the million-dollar question. I assume it's

Dimitri. Could it have been he who caused mine, all those years ago?" Kir says.

It doesn't seem likely, but nothing surprises me anymore.

"Or…" Niko says, "maybe Dimitri isn't behind Stacey's crash. Maybe we need to widen our focus?"

Kir gets to his feet again, clearly tortured, and gazes out the window to our south lawn. "Look at her out there. It's like she's training for the Olympics or something."

Niko and I join him at the window to watch Charleigh with her trainer.

That's one of the problems with the business we're in. You never know who's coming for you.

CHAPTER SIX

Vadik

We would have preferred to use our own resources to keep Charleigh safe, rather than have her trained to defend herself. I wish no situation would ever arise where she had to take up for herself, where she was on her own without us to take care of our her the way we should. But the reality is, this shit does happen, it has happened, and it could very well happen again.

What really killed me is that the first time we suggested training, she jumped all over the idea, insisting she start right away, as if she knew we couldn't keep her safe and that she really was on her own in the world. That stung. And now, every day she relives the brutal treatment she suffered at the hands of Dimitri and his men. She might be getting stronger physically, but emotionally, she's so drawn into herself I'm afraid we may have lost her.

The only time I see a little light in her eyes is when her sister comes in the room. But I know she's putting on a show for Evie.

She's just dead on the inside.

The question is, can we bring her back to life?

I'm lying if I don't admit this haunts me. I never realized someone else's pain could become my own, maybe aside from my brothers, and yet here we are. To survive, I've thrown myself into work like I always do. It's my escape, it always has been, whenever the stress is getting too much to take.

Mama always said I was a workaholic. Papa said I was ambitious. But the truth falls somewhere in between the two. If you bury yourself in work, there are a lot of other things in life you don't have to focus on, things you can avoid. Seems I've become quite the champ at that.

Granted, I've always been a hard worker. I wanted to make my parents proud, ensure the family name remains respected, and continue the work my father started as an immigrant in this country. It wasn't easy for him, although he never complained. It seems the least I—and my brothers—can do is honor his legacy by keeping the businesses he started strong and successful.

With these self-imposed pressures, I've never had much time for anything other than work. No relationships, no hobbies—none of that bullshit.

Kir, he has his cooking. Or he did. Once he lost Clara, he stopped doing anything that reminded him of her. But he's an amazing amateur chef, so yeah, he can have life outside work when he wants to.

Niko's always been the playboy out of the three of us. I wouldn't peg him as a man-whore, not by a long shot, but the girls like him and he likes them right back. He typically has dates several nights a week. Well, he did until Charleigh came along.

But me, I've always been pretty much about work. I don't take vacations, go to any more parties than I absolutely have to, and only spend time with women who are as eager to get their rocks off as I am. Nothing more. They usually do it for money. Keeps it simpler that way.

This sort of life has served me well for a long time. But something's different now. I'm not sure I like it.

In fact, I know I don't. It's uncomfortable, like a too-small pair of shoes you can't take off.

Lately, work has not been the soothing balm for me it was the past. When my parents died, I barely left the office, and when I did, it was only to sleep three or four hours after several drinks. It was how I got through those tough days without losing my mind.

But now, not even work is protecting me from myself. Which means Charleigh's on my mind pretty much all fucking day and night.

No one knows except security—and they'll never say anything if they want to keep their jobs and their lives—but I've been checking in on Charleigh several times a night just to make sure she's still fucking there. We've almost lost her so many times now, I feel like our luck just might be running out, something I thought I'd never say, and that the next time she's in danger, we might not get her back.

How the fuck does someone get the better of the Alekseev brothers? Are we losing our hold on our power structure? Are other factions testing us to a greater extent than before? Have we been attacked so many times now we're seen as weak? Do others believe that with the loss of our father comes the fall of the Alekseev empire?

Fuck that.

Not possible. And if anyone wants to argue about it, I'll cut their head right off. We might have recently suffered serious blows, but that's to be expected in our world. There are always ups and downs, and we will strike back, but at the right time. Not a moment sooner. Anyone who sees in us a sign of weakness for biding our time is a fool setting himself up for a big surprise. One of the reasons the Alekseevs are as strong as we are is that we take action with great forethought—we never strike first chance we get. We usually wait, gage the situation, and devise a harsh and merciless strike. Everyone knows that about us. They respect it. They fear it.

Impulsivity? That's for amateurs, newbies, and brash idiots. Not that I don't have the occasional blind urge, the desire to off someone who's done me wrong. I just know to control it. Strike at the optimal time.

In spite of my distractions, I keep reminding myself it should be a load off my mind that we've brought on new security. And I am glad Charleigh's self-defense training is building her confidence. Hopefully, my brothers and I can protect her so that she never needs it, but if it makes her feel better, I'm all for it.

The Charleigh we knew before the attack is not the Charleigh we have right now. She's a remnant of her former self, obsessed with revenge to a greater extent than I think I've ever seen. And I've spent a lot of time around people seeking revenge. It will consume you with its insidious tentacles, trap you in its bitterness, and rob you of any light you ever carried. It nearly destroyed me when my parents were murdered, like a sick obsession. But two years has helped me mellow, and the belief that we'll eventually get my parents' killers makes it easier to get through the day.

"Do you… do you think she's overdoing it?" Niko asks, frowning.

I know she hit him the other day when he tried to kiss her. On one hand, I guess it's understandable. On the other, it's pretty fucked up.

I'm surprised by her warrior mindset. Never would have thought she had it in her. I'd hate to be on her bad side.

The woman is seriously determined to make a bitch pay.

"I definitely think she's overdoing it with the training. Not so much physically, but mentally for sure. And she's insisting on firearms training now," Kir says. "It's great she's getting in shape and all that, but she's getting fanatical about it."

Niko shakes his head. "He thought *we* were after his ass, but he ought to *really* be scared now," he says with an ironic laugh. "He pissed off the wrong woman."

CHAPTER SEVEN

Vadik

An hour later, when Charleigh's training is done if not for the day, then at least for the time being, we file into her room while she's in the shower.

"Um. What are you guys doing here?" she asks when she gets out, tightening the sash on her robe, her hair dripping water onto the floor.

"We want to talk to you," I say. "Would you mind having a seat?"

She looks from one of us to the next, suspicious, clearly having lost all ability to trust.

I get it. I can't say I'm a trusting person, not by a long shot, but to see someone as guileless as her change almost overnight comes as a surprise to even a cynical bastard like me.

She takes a seat on the easy chair in the corner of the room, about as far away from the three of us as possible.

If that's what she needs to do, fine.

"What's going on with you, Charleigh?" Kir asks.

Her head twitches and she frowns like she doesn't understand the question. Yeah, right. I call bullshit. She knows full well what we are getting at. She's not a stupid woman. There's no way she hasn't seen the change in herself, nor would she expect anyone else to overlook it.

"Are you going to pretend you're the same person you were before your attack? Or can we talk about how it's affected you?" I ask.

Might as well rip the bandage right off.

She looks down at her hands and begins to pick her cuticles. Which is good. She's listening. Reflecting.

"We can talk about whatever you want to talk about," she says in a flat, bored voice.

Okay. She's not rolling over for us. Didn't expect her to, really.

"Charleigh, we're afraid you're taking this training thing a little too far. We *will* get Dimitri. He *will* pay for what he's done. Don't doubt that. Don't doubt *us*. But what are you going to do once we have gotten him? Are you going to keep this up for the rest of your life?"

She clicks her tongue and rolls her eyes like a petulant kid on the defense. "You guys are just mad because I'm not 'servicing' you anymore," she says, using air quotes.

What?

Fuck all, if that wasn't a strike below the belt.

So not necessary. And such bullshit.

Before I can think of a way to respond without losing my temper, Niko jumps to his feet, his face red. He lopes toward her like an angry bull and she recoils, I notice with her hands in closed fists. She's ready to take him on, not that she wants to. She's just gotten to where this is her automatic response.

Regardless, I can't recall ever seeing my brother angry, much less *this* angry.

"That's bullshit and you know it," he growls. "Stop acting like you're our whore. You know we don't see you that way, goddammit."

Her eyes widen at his scolding, and her own face begins to redden. Then her eyes fill with tears, which she quickly wipes away with the sleeve of her bathrobe. The new Charleigh is all about hiding her emotions.

She got the reaction out of Niko she wanted. She

won't get it from me, though. I have more control than my younger brother, for better or for worse, and I can see right through her tough talk. Underneath it is a lovely young woman who's suffering. Badly.

What I want her to learn, to understand, is that when she suffers, we suffer too.

Finally, a tear trickles down her cheek. "I was powerless. You couldn't protect me, Frank couldn't protect me, nobody could protect me. I'm not letting that happen again. I'm taking back my power. If I ever had any to begin with." This is when she starts to cry harder. "No one's ever taken up for me. I've always been alone. And I'm tired of it."

Against my better judgment, I jump to my feet and am across the room in two long steps. I take her by the arms and pull her to me. She needs to feel the protection we offer her.

And to know each of us would sacrifice our own lives to keep her safe, given the chance.

But she isn't ready. "Let me go!" she screams.

I don't. I can't. I pull her tighter. She fights me harder.

Kir's hand lands on my shoulder, warning me to loosen my grip. But I can't seem to. I want her to know how important she is and how much she means to me. I've got to get her to listen. I've got to get through to her.

I can't deny my feelings for this woman. They're uncomfortable, painful, revelatory, and insidious. I don't do things like this, fall for women, especially women like Charleigh. I'll be the ruin of her.

If I haven't already.

CHAPTER EIGHT

Charleigh

When I realize I don't stand a chance against Vadik, I stop trying to push him away. Why waste the energy? I'm already worn out by today's workout.

And his touch isn't as bad as I thought it might be. I'd been dreading physical contact with anyone, even my sister, but Vadik's hands are big, strong, and warm. And his eyes are full of caring. Say what you want about him, he is not a heartless monster. It just takes a little work to get beyond his thick, scaly exterior.

But I still have my limits and can't make myself hold his gaze. It's just too... uncomfortable. I'm looking anywhere but at his face, and he's only inches from mine. If he wants more connection than

I can give at this moment, he'll have to go without. I'm not here for him that way, not today.

I'm like a big piece of glass with a crack down the middle. I can be repaired, maybe, but I also might crumble to pieces. I don't know which. Neither do the guys. This weighs on them, I can tell. On one hand, I'm fortunate to have someone worrying about me. Most of my life, that has not been the case. But on the other, it's a shitload of responsibility. I can feel the weight of it on my shoulders. I don't want to let them down, and the pressure has been pushing me away.

We're all hurting, but I can't take care of them right now. They have to rely on their own resources. My distancing may feel hostile and cold, but I'm in survival mode and for the time being, they'll just have to take care of themselves. I can't take on their pain. I couldn't if I wanted to.

I'm just getting by, for Christ's sake. If it weren't for my sister, I'm not even sure I'd bother.

In spite of myself, I can't help but let my eyes flutter closed when Vadik's lips land on my damp neck. He pushes wet strings of hair off my skin and it's actually reassuring, like taking a deep breath after swimming the length of a pool under water. His kisses are calming, as if he's telling me with his body that things will be okay.

In time.

Or maybe that's the story I'm telling myself, one I've told myself so many times before. I am pretty sure I've lost my old optimism, but maybe there's still a smidgeon somewhere deep inside, which Vadik is drawing out by taking on some of the pain that has so overwhelmed me.

His brothers settle in across the room, taking seats for themselves, and it dawns on me they are *here* for me. Like, *really* here for me. Not just physically, but also emotionally. They're taking on some of my hurt so I can get ahead of it and maybe even at some point beat it off. That's caring.

So I step away from Vadik and walk to the middle of the room. I drop my robe and stand there defiantly, stark naked, for all to see, and turn, finally making eye contact with each of the brothers. I'm not saying my unease, the itchiness I feel in my own skin, is gone or forgotten, but a little twist of desire, of want, has heated up inside me and it's telling me to go with it, that the guys won't hurt me and in fact will make me feel quite good if I let them.

And that I might enjoy making them feel good, as well.

"Come closer," I say.

In seconds, I am surrounded by the three most beautiful men I've ever laid eyes on. Their dangerous good looks never stop amazing me, every damn time I look at them. To be honest, it takes my breath away that God made men so stunning and that for many godforsaken reasons, my life path has crossed with theirs. It's looking like ours may be infinitely entwined, whether I want that or not.

On my left is Kir, whose thick black hair just brushes his shoulders, a small rebellion against his brothers' more buttoned-up styles. Placing my hand on the back of his neck, I step closer, until our lips touch. His kiss is gritty and rough and demanding just like he is, and his fists knead the flesh of my ass so hard I know he'll leave bruises.

He makes me feel alive.

Directly in front of me is Niko, the charmer of the three Alekseev men, able to negotiate his way out of all manner of difficult situations just by order of his patient, easy-going persona. He's young, closer to my age than the other guys, and we crack shared jokes about the music and TV shows of our time. I run my nails along his jawline facial scruff and settle them into his dirty blond hair, for once not sweeping aside the lock that always seems to fall into his face. The kiss he gives me is sensual, luxurious, and unhurried. When our tongues meet, my nipples stiffen even though the room's grown warm.

He makes me feel safe.

Vadik stands on my right, and I return to kissing him the way I meant to just moments before. I draw back for a moment and run my finger down his crooked nose and he laughs, we all laugh, and he grabs a hank of my hair and pulls me to him for a deep, soul-clenching kiss, one that releases all the butterflies in my stomach that have been cocooned for too long. I run my open palms over his shaved head and remember what he looked like with a head of thick black hair like his brother Kir, which I saw in those strange photos from Dominika's locker.

He makes me feel scared. In a good way.

Kir has started removing his jacket and tie, followed by Niko, and the way the men look at me is with so much desire it scares me for a moment, thinking I could never be what they want me to, could never measure up to their expectations.

But that's to worry about another day because we're here right now and I am enough, in fact, I'm more than enough. Dimitri and his gang might have inflicted their pain on me, both physically and mentally, but they haven't stolen my soul, and this is something I need to reassure the Alekseev brothers of.

I back up toward my bed and when I reach it, take a seat and slide back. I fluff a pillow under my head because I want to watch everything, everything these men do to me. I spread my legs, and run one finger though my pussy in invitation. As if they need one.

I nearly come because I haven't touched myself in so long, my desire having been deadened, and now I'm hyper-sensitive, and it's fucking delicious. With the guys' attentions on me, I lift my hips to grind against my hand, and slide one finger inside myself.

"Holy fuck," Kir says, joining me on the bed. "You wanna suck some cock, baby?" he asks.

I smile and laugh, because of course I do. He inches up to where my head rests on a pillow and straddles my face like he's about to fuck it. But before I take his cock, I let his balls fall to my mouth, where I lick and tease them, just to torment him a bit.

After, I grip his hard cock and direct it to my lips, where I taste his first drop of salty precum, then slide his head past my lips, where I give him a swirl of my tongue.

"Fuck yeah," he grunts, pulsing his hips.

While I can't see behind Kir, I know Vadik's hands are on my thighs. He runs his tongue between my pussy lips, and I shudder from the sensation. He presses my thighs further apart and holds them there. I still manage to buck my hips despite his restraining me.

With Kir fucking my face and Vadik between my legs, I want still more and have an idea. I push Kir out of my mouth and off my face, and Vadik stops too.

I scramble to my knees. "Kir, lay down so I can get on top," I say, pointing at the bed.

He smiles knowingly and a moment later, I'm sliding down his cock, my pussy full to its maximum. I lean with my head in the crook of his neck, my butt in the air. After licking my finger, I swirl it around my asshole as best as I can reach.

"Fuck. Would you look at that," Niko groans.

That's right. I know what I want. I know what I need. And I'd better get it soon or I will lose my mind.

"Baby, baby," he says, getting behind me. He pushes my hand out of the way and takes over, dribbling spit on my rosebud. He presses against my opening, massaging and prodding, and works a finger inside. The sensation is surprising but after a few seconds starts to feel amazing. I explode in goosebumps.

I continue to grind on Kir's cock, my clit rubbing against his stomach. I'm careful not to displace Niko with my movement, and when he pops another finger in my ass, I nearly lose my mind.

I push back on him for more. I can't help it

because I need to explode, to detonate, to forget who or where I am. I want to be fucked so hard I pass out into a dreamless sleep where I don't worry about my problems again until the light of day, where everything is bright and happy and I feel no pain, no pain in my muscles or my brain or my heart.

As if he can hear my chaotic thinking, Niko presses something new against my behind, something much bigger than a finger or two. It's hard and round, and it's pushing and pushing until it pops inside, initially hurting like hell. I grind my teeth and groan while Kir whispers in my ear that the discomfort will pass.

"I don't know, Kir, I don't know if I can take it," I cry, pounding the pillow next to his head.

Goddammit.

A cock in my ass and a cock in my pussy? How is that even possible?

He takes hold of my head and catches my gaze. "You can do it, push out a bit and take deep breaths."

Niko gently stays where he is while something cold dribbles down my butt. He rubs it around and after a little more pulsing, which I am growing to love, he slides further inside.

Full doesn't begin to explain the feeling of being fucked in two holes. I can't see or think straight. I know a massive orgasm is building and every inch of me is so stimulated, so sensitive it almost hurts, like if someone touches me, my flesh will split open like an overripe piece of fruit.

This build and builds until I'm gasping for air and I don't know who I am anymore, and I don't care either. I explode into a level of ecstasy I didn't know existed, my pussy and ass both contracting, doubling down on me, pushing me to the very edges of my already-tenuous sanity.

"More," I murmur like a crazy bitch, bucking into both of the cocks that have taken me.

Kir holds my face. "Tell me, baby, is it good? Do you like being double-fucked?"

I grunt, wishing I could verbalize an answer. But words are elusive at the moment, so I nod, my hair flying all over.

I come over and over, floating on my orgasm like it's a life raft that will save me, save me from the shit all around me, and maybe even save me from myself.

I'm not sure how long the guys hang out after our sexy session, but after one of them helps me clean up with a warm washcloth, I tumble into my bed like it's heaven. My down comforter is pulled up to my chin and I fall into a deep, deep sleep, eternally grateful to know I can be touched without flashing back to the last time I was, when Dimitri's team beat me to within an inch of my life to send a lesson to the Alekseev brothers.

I didn't know whether I would survive that day, and when it comes down to it, Dimitri probably should have made sure I was dead because I healed stronger and tougher than I knew I could, like scar tissue that grows around and over a wound. I'm not saying they could never hurt me again, but if they try, it's not going to be as easy as it was, that much I know for sure.

CHAPTER NINE

Charleigh

Was last night all a dream? The feeling of perfect being that accompanied me to sleep is, unfortunately, fading as fast as the morning sun is coming up in my bedroom window.

Dammit.

I push myself up and look around my room. There is no sign of anyone else having been in here. The only mess is a pile of texts and notebooks on my desk, which haven't been touched in weeks and are now dusty. I look away, the reminder of my neglected courses too painful.

I don't need another thing about myself to detest.

Then I get an idea. I jump out of bed, gathering all evidence of my former ambition into my arms. I find a place in the way back of my closet and shove all my books and notebooks there so I don't have to look at them and be reminded of how my life has gotten so off track. I'll get back to them someday, I imagine, but right now I don't need these things out in the open, reminding me that the dream I once had of a better life has been burned to the ground. I don't know what lies ahead anymore. I can only focus on a day at a time.

I'm pulling on my workout clothes when there's a knock on my door.

"Char? It's me, Evie."

"Hey. Come in," I call.

She pokes her head into the room, looking around as if she expects to see someone other than me.

"Char, were you having sex last night?" she asks, closing the door after she enters.

Oops.

"Yes, I was. Sorry about the noise," I say, trying to keep things completely normal while I pull on my sock and sneakers.

Her eyes widen like she caught me at something and I wait for a smart-ass remark or two.

"Was it fun?" she teases, sauntering around my room, touching this and that like I'm really going to share details with her.

Not.

"Yes, it was fun, Evie. It was great. I loved it. Is there anything else you want to know?"

She's trying not to smile, like she's all grown up and stuff, but she giggles, either out of embarrassment or nervousness, or both.

"What about you, Evie. Have you had sex yet?" I ask.

God, I hope she didn't do anything with that creep relative of Dimitris's.

Her gaze whips in my direction, and she looks like she'd rather die than have this conversation with me.

But hell, she brought it up.

"Come here, Evie," I say, patting the bed next to me. "Have a seat."

She does, staring at her hands and picking at her chipped black nail polish.

"Have you? You can tell me," I say.

She takes a deep breath. "No. I was going to. With that guy Arseny. He was really bugging me for it. But I wanted to wait for the right time and place. Thank God I didn't," she says, her voice breaking a little.

I stroke her hair, then start to braid it like our mother used to. "I'm sorry how all that turned out. I'm glad you found out the kind of person he was before it was too late."

She sniffles and nods. "How could I have been so stupid?"

I take her chin and turn her toward me. "You liked him because he was nice to you. Until he wasn't. He's a bad guy from a family of bad guys. You had no way of knowing."

She nods and her sad face reminds me of when she was six and our mother was gone. I had to try so hard to get her to eat a peanut butter and jelly sandwich. When she did, just to please me, she nearly choked, that's how badly she didn't want it, and ten years later I still feel horrible for trying to force her.

"You know what, honey? You're going to be okay. Our lives are crazy right now, but they won't always be. And with the guys looking out for us, there will be no more Arsenys to get within a hundred yards of you before they tell him to take a hike."

She laughs a little. "Char?"

"Yeah?"

"I… I won't make that mistake again," she says, like she's so old and wise.

If only I believed her.

"One other thing, Char."

"Yeah?"

She swallows hard. "Well, um, Char, I want to move back home. With Pops. I miss my old life."

Holy shit, I did not see that coming.

She looks up at me with her big, sad eyes and my heart breaks knowing I have to keep her here, that the Alekseev compound is the only safe place for the two of us, even though no teenager should have to live like she's in a prison, even in a nice one like we have here.

I sigh and rub her back. "You know that's not going to happen, Evie. I'm sorry. I wish things were different."

She squirms, throwing my hand off her.

Punk.

"Did Pops really sell you to these guys? Is that why you can't leave?" she suddenly asks, her eyes drilling mine like she's daring me to lie.

My God.

"Where did you hear that?"

She shrugs. "I heard bit and pieces. I sort of put the story together."

I look around the room, wondering where to start. "Look Evie, someday I will tell you the whole story, but Pops got into some financial trouble. It was… decided that I'd go to work for the guys. I waitressed for a while until… they said I didn't have to anymore. And I've been here, with them, since. They feel it's safer. Just like it is for you."

Skeptical, she frowns. "Do you like them?"

Hmmm. How to answer that. "They have their good sides. So, I guess I could say I'm still deciding."

If only I believed that. Any decision to be made already has been. They might have kidnapped or stolen me, or whatever the hell our arrangement can be called, but they've also stolen my heart, and that's not something I'm going to get back.

CHAPTER TEN

Kir

"The *Pakhan* wants to meet with you."

Charleigh frowns, playing with the locker around her neck. "What? *Me*? Why?" she asks, trying but failing to hide the tremble in her voice.

I knew she wouldn't be happy about this. After all, last time she was in front of the *Pakhan,* he dismissed her as an inconsequential female, as he does all women. Someone who grew up in our world might be used to such treatment by the older, more traditional men in the syndicate, but to Charleigh, it was pretty fucking insulting.

It pissed her off. Actually, she's been pissed off a lot lately.

She needs to control her anger when she's with

him. She can vent with us guys, afterwards, but trying to put the *Pakhan* in his place is a waste of breath at the very least, and downright dangerous to her, at worst. If the man hasn't learned by now that women deserve more respect than his generation doles out, Charleigh certainly isn't going to change his ways, much as she'd like to.

I speak slowly, hoping to calm her nerves. "He wants to hear your version of what happened with Dimitri. He listens to both sides and then decides how he wants to settle matters," I say like this is business as usual.

I know this won't placate her. She has no patience for the *Pakhan* deciding anything. But if she doesn't bide her time, she won't accomplish a thing, and she'll never get close to the revenge that is driving her soul right now. We've got to get that through to her.

Her fingers drill the arm of the chair she's in, and she shifts like she's uncomfortable. "*You* already told him everything. I have nothing to add."

I reach for her hand. "It will be fine. He'll be perfectly nice. Take it as a compliment, that he wants to hear the story straight from you. That shows he believes you."

Her eyes widen. "He *believes me*? Was there ever

any question? We know exactly who took me, what they did to me, and why. Are you saying he needs some sort of convincing or something?"

The pitch of her voice rises as she speaks faster and faster.

She throws her arms up. "What more can I tell him? I mean, does he think I made the whole thing up?"

I shake my head. "It's not like that, Charleigh."

She juts her chin out. "What if I don't *want* to meet with him? He's… a scary man. And besides, *I* know what Dimitri did, and that's all that matters. And I know what I'm going to do to him in return. So who cares what the *Pakhan* says."

I try not to laugh. What she is saying makes perfect sense.

Just not in our world.

"What's a *Pakhan,* anyway?" she asks rolling her eyes.

It dawns on me that for as long as she's been with us, she knows next to nothing about the organization. She hasn't needed to, but since she's asking, I'll tell her the bare minimum she needs. Not sure how my brothers will feel about this, but they're across the room, letting me take the lead.

I speak before they can interrupt me. "He's basically the head guy, the head of several factions, anyway. The Bratva tends to be flatter than other organized… groups. That way, if something goes wrong, there's always somebody to take over. We're never caught without a leader. We're harder to dismantle that way."

She looks at me like I'm crazy. Maybe I am.

I decide to give her a little context. "Russia's organized crime pretty much started during the imperial times, when we had tsars and such. The rift between the haves and have-nots was beyond extreme. Some took from the rich and gave to the poor like Robin Hood, and an organized method for doing that came into being. They were folk heroes in their day."

She furrows her brow. "Are you serious? Is that a true story?"

"That's how I always heard it from my papa. I mean, it makes sense. It's part of what brought Imperial Russia down. You know, Nicolas and Alexandra?"

She looks at me blankly.

I'm no expert in Russian history. Hell, I've never even been there. After Mama and Papa came to the US, they couldn't have gone back if they wanted to. Apparently, Papa left behind some people who didn't like him very much. There was a price on his head, which meant never seeing the old country again.

When it came down to it, though, I'm not so sure he missed it. Here in the US, he built a life surrounded by other Russians in the same situation. It's like he brought a piece of the land with him but with less danger and more opportunity. He exploited those opportunities every chance he got and made it into the empire my brothers and I run today. Some people would never approve of what he had to do to get buy, but they can suck my dick. We provide products and services that are in demand. Very high demand.

It's not hard to see that Charleigh has absorbed all the history she cares to for one day. She's antsy, not happy with unfinished business hanging over her head, and isn't buying my plea for patience. I know how she's thinking. I've seen it a hundred times, and it never works out the way people think it will. She wants to just walk up to Dimitri and put a bullet to his head. To her, that's the end of things, and a new beginning for her.

I mean sure, she could do that, but she'd just end up facing a dozen other problems. We have our ways of doing things, and if we follow protocol, things will be resolved to her satisfaction. If we don't, a tit-for-tat response will consume all parties, and there will be more people left dead than not.

Of course, Charleigh wants to hear none of this. I can't blame her, so our job, for the time being, is to keep her focused and out of trouble.

She crosses her arms tightly. "I don't want to wait for the *Pakhan's* blessing. I don't need it. He's nobody to me. I'm not part of his or your *Bratva* world, so I don't give a shit what he says about anything."

My brothers and I look at each other. If she doesn't get it now, she never will. That's the difference between someone brought up in our world, and someone brought up outside it.

I hate to see her like this, obsessed with something a girl like her was never meant to be confronted with. The attack by Dimitri killed something in her, and I don't like it. None of us do. The light in her eyes is dimmer, and the spring in her step is pretty much gone. Her voice is nearly always flat, and she just picks at the food on her plate.

What angers me the most about this is that Dimitri didn't just steal something big from Charleigh. He took it from us, too.

Which was the whole fucking point.

So yeah, I'd like to see the fucker on his knees, begging for mercy with tears running down his face and snot leaking from his nose before one of us explodes his skull with a bullet. I'd like to see that right now. Maybe even more than Charleigh does.

But it will happen, in due time. He'll never get away with what he did and what he took from us.

Because what he took, we may never get back. The guileless young woman who enchanted my brothers and me could very well be gone forever.

Meaning this will be the second woman I've lost. I'm not sure I can take that again.

My own issues aside, no one is suffering more than our Charleigh. It's like there's no containing the anger seeping from her pores, and the consequences of rash choices—like killing Dimitri *now*—seem mild compared to what she's carrying around. There is no hiding it, her suffering, wearing it on her sleeve as she does. We stalled on setting up her meeting with the *Pakhan* as long as we could, using her injuries as an excuse, because there's no telling whether she'll listen to him quietly as he expects, or lose her shit all over him.

Things could go right… or terribly wrong. There's no controlling her, much as we've tried to. When Dimitri messed with Charleigh, he bought an enemy for life, adding to the roster of people who'd like to see him leave this earth.

What not only worries us about Charleigh not knowing our customs and saying the wrong thing, is also the knowledge of the deal she's likely to be offered by the *Pakhan*—one where she walks away and forgets the attack ever happened because he offers her a large sum of money. That's how he resolves things. We know that and accept it.

But clearly, the *Pakhan* doesn't know our girl.

All the money in the universe would not sway her convictions.

Ever.

So my brothers and I have to balance this, which could turn ugly because two strong-willed people won't be getting what they want.

The bottom line, which the *Pakhan* is going to find out, is that Charleigh can't be bought. Problem is, he's not used to negotiating with women. As in, he probably never has had to, not in his entire life. She'll make the case, asking how safe will she really ever be with Dimitri still alive, but I doubt that will sway him, and if he feels he's being challenged or disrespected, things will quickly go south.

Across the room I see Niko lean forward in his chair, hands clasped, in his best negotiating posture. "We know the *Pakhan* means nothing to you, Charleigh. But we need you to do this for us? Will you? For us?"

What can I say? The man has skills.

She looks around the room, obviously not happy.

"I guess," she says with a drawn-out sigh. "Yeah, I'll meet with him. I mean, what choice do I have?"

She's starting to get it

Vadik slaps his thigh and gets to his feet. "You're right, baby. You really do have no choice," he says, signaling the meeting is over.

CHAPTER ELEVEN

KIR

"You can't blame yourselves," Charleigh says, picking at her salad.

Does she really mean that? Or is she just blowing smoke up our asses? I can tell my brothers are thinking the same thing.

She sets her fork aside after eating half a tomato. Jesus, if her appetite doesn't come back soon, she won't live long enough to see Dimitri taken out. I want to ask her how many pounds she's lost but I know better than to bring up a woman's weight. Talk about kicking a hornet's nest.

It's clear she's put a lot of thought into this. I'm glad she's talking responsibility. She may not know it yet, but she's going to be part of our lives for a long, long time. She has to know how her actions have consequences.

She rubs her neck. "You didn't expect me to go to the arcade that day. In fact, I had to talk Frank into it, something I regret terribly. We didn't know Dimitri was setting a trap. Neither did you guys. I had an awesome bodyguard and they still got me. Bottom line, no one can protect me, except me."

Not sure I like the way that sounds, but there is a lot of truth to it. Staying safe starts with making smart decisions. Keep out of the line of fire, so to speak. If she keeps doing crazy-ass, impetuous things, well, that won't end well. Not at all.

This makes my stomach churn, and I set my coffee down. I couldn't protect Clara. And now, Charleigh. What good are all the precautions in the world if we can't do something that simple?

She continues. "I… I don't mean to hurt you by saying that. You are powerful men, but not everything is in your control. I have free will, at least to an extent, and the decision I made put me in danger. The most important thing I've learned in my self-defense course is to not take a stupid risk to begin with. Staying out of dangerous situations is seventy-five percent of protecting yourself. The other twenty-five, well, we'll see if I can physically defend myself if I ever need to. Still working on that." She laughs sadly.

That's huge progress. Our girl is learning. And she's right. If she can follow what she's been learning, it's unlikely anything like this will happen to her again. There is no guarantee, but smart thinking reduces the chances.

Vadik joins us at the table, late. "Okay," he says, settling in, "just talked to the *Pakhan*'s second. What a miserable son of a bitch. Anyway, we're all set for our meeting, but the bastard wouldn't give me a read on what to expect."

So typical of that power-hungry loser. He loves nothing more than lording the little bit of power he has over people. Why the *Pakhan* keeps him on is beyond me, but someday he'll get his due. People like him always do.

"You didn't get to speak directly to the *Pakhan*?" Charleigh asks.

Vadik shakes his head. "Nope. Are you kidding, with that boot-licking gatekeeper in the way? But don't worry, darlin', we'll protect you. We'll make sure you're okay every step of the way."

Charleigh grimaces, no doubt the thought of having to protect herself running through her mind. She doesn't trust us guys anymore.

That kills me.

She was hurt on my watch. I don't know how I'll ever forgive myself. While I haven't discussed it with my brothers, my guess is they feel the same. Were I to ask him, Niko would readily admit his regrets. Vadik, not so much. Not that he doesn't have any, it's just harder for him to talk about some things.

"You know, guys, when I was being held by Dimitri, I don't remember much, but I do recall there being a room he went in and out of a bunch of times. He had a key and I didn't see anyone else going in there. It must be something super confidential. Like, maybe there's info about what he did to your parents in there?" she says matter-of-factly.

That's our new Charleigh. Everything is matter-of-fact. No real emotion. Like the wonderment has been completely beaten out of her.

At least we still have her, though. I feel like I've been given a second chance, something I never had with Clara.

Vadik sucks in a deep breath. "Who the fuck knows what he's up to. But I can tell you one thing. He's so fucking dead..." he says, gritting his teeth.

I couldn't have said it better myself.

"You know, Charleigh, I feel like you should know that when you first went missing, we assumed you'd run away again," Niko says with regret in his eyes. "We quickly figured out there was foul play. But that was our first thought."

It's just like Niko to have to confess shit. If he were any more sensitive, he'd be a goddamn girl.

Her shoulders slump, and damn if that doesn't break my heart a little. "I don't blame you. The first time I went missing, I *had* run, so why shouldn't you suspect it again?"

We're quiet while Chef takes away our dishes. It's odd that Charleigh is here at the club without her sister, she so seldom leaves her anymore, but Evie must be with Gloria, who's taken to helping her with her lessons. It's funny, the very same housekeeper used to help Niko. It was hard for her when my parents died, having been with them so many years, but our household help were taken care of while we rebuilt. We needed their loyalty, and well, money can buy a shit ton of that.

"You all were rough on me when I came back from running off, and to be honest, I was going to leave again at some point, only with better planning. But then Evie started getting into trouble, and she became my priority. Now I realize I can't leave no matter how much I might want to." She closes her eyes and takes a deep breath. "I can never leave, now. There is a price on my head. There always will be."

CHAPTER TWELVE

CHARLEIGH

"The Alekseevs will wait here. You come with me, Miss Gates."

The *Pakhan's* second, as the guys call him, is gesturing at me to follow. But he can kiss my ass.

I look at the brothers. They've got to do something. They promised to protect me. And there can't be anything more dangerous than leaving me alone with the *Pakhan* and his creepy associate. I mean, talk about throwing someone to the wolves.

I stand, happy I wore the highest heels I have. They kill my feet but make me feel like a serious bad-ass babe.

And I need all the bad-ass vibes I can get.

I approach the second, closer than I want to be to

him, but I have a point to make. A very clear point. "I'm going nowhere without the guys. Sorry."

I tilt my head defiantly, hoping like hell he doesn't notice my shaking hands.

The guys have noticed though, and while they look cool, I know they're ready to jump this asshole. In fact, there is probably nothing they'd like more, at the moment.

"I am sorry, lady. He says *you*. Alone," he sneers back at me, smugness seeping from every pore.

I get it. This guy, and all the Bratva I guess, aren't accustomed to women challenging them. It's obvious. But that doesn't mean I'm just going to bend over for them.

Sorry, not sorry.

To prove my point, I go back to my chair and plop down, ignoring the second like he's not even in the room. And as I do, I spot Niko and Vadik reflexively touching their guns under their suit jackets. I've become accustomed to this subtle movement. I've grown to find it strangely comforting, just like I suppose they do.

The only thing that would be more comforting would be if I had my own firearm.

The tension in the room over my stand-off grows, with the second insisting I come with him alone, and my insisting on only going if the guys can come with me. I don't know how this is going to shake out, but I act like I don't give a shit by looking around the room and occasionally examining my cuticles.

Like I haven't a concern in the world.

Nope. Just another day at the office.

Niko gets to his feet and approaches the second, patting him on the back like they're buddies who can easily come to an agreement.

The second doesn't see it that way and stiffens at Niko's touch.

"Charleigh's been through a lot," Niko says by way of explanation, "and the *Pakhan* knows that. He'll understand. Now, shall we get the show on the road rather than make the man wait?"

The second's expression is unchanging, like he's some sort of ugly Russian robot.

I don't wait to be left alone with the *Pakhan,* nor his second. I find it hard enough to trust the Alekseev brothers anymore, doing so only because I don't have much of a choice. One of the men from their world hurt me, and I know others are perfectly willing to. Women aren't valued by men like the *Pakhan*. We're little more than chattel. Everything about my self-defense training says *not* to put oneself in a dangerous situation to begin with. And yet here I am, walking into the lion's den.

The second's phone beeps and he pulls it to his ear, continuing to keep an eye on the four of us. "Yes, sir?" he says. "She's coming right away. Yes, sir. Thank you."

He drops his phone back into the pocket of his ill-fitting suit and reaches to pat his weapon just like the brothers do.

"Lady, come," he grunts.

What the hell. Is this how things end? We have a standoff and then everyone shoots each other dead?

What is with these men? They're dangerous and scary but also sometimes incredibly fucking stupid.

I slowly push myself to my feet, like it's a great bother. It's clear I'm putting all of us in danger with my refusal to budge. Sure, I might end up in a difficult situation alone with the *Pakhan,* but in the interest of minimizing collateral damage, I cave. I consent to the second's demand.

Like I ever had a choice.

"Fine. Let's go. I'm ready," I sigh, my posture strong as I fight the heaviness in my chest.

The heaviness I've been fighting for weeks.

I'll go meet with the *Pakhan.* On my own. I'll show him the carving on my stomach. I'll show him the lump where my broken clavicle healed unevenly. I'll show him the scar hidden by my hair, where I was hit with something that split my head open.

Seems that's the only way to communicate with him. If he wants to see proof of what happened to me, I'll fucking show him some.

I have no idea what this man has in store for me, but these recent weeks have been about conquering my fears. I'm strong, stronger than I have ever been, and I will face whatever shit comes my way. If, God forbid, something happens to me, I am comforted knowing the guys will look after Evie until she's eighteen. They know sending her back to my father is not an option.

We leave the guys, a heavy door closing behind the second and me, and enter a long hallway. I am alone with him against my better judgement, against the guys' better judgement, and it doesn't feel good. I've only ever seen this guy around the club, usually with Dimitri, and it's clear he's trouble. Before I even knew anything about the world I'm now immersed in, I knew to watch my back around him, that's now much slime oozes off him.

He might be loyal to his boss, the *Pakhan,* but he's crazy like all these other men. And crazy comes with unpredictability. I might not have a firearm like all these guys do, something that makes me feel invincible, but I've managed to… *acquire* a little something that may come in handy. Just like the second and the brothers pat their jackets for reassurance that their firearms are close by, I pat my own pocket for comfort, where I've stashed a stiletto knife. The one my self-defense instructor was showing me how to use.

Which he doesn't know I swiped from him.

The man was teaching me knife skills the other day. At the end of our session, he was packing up his stuff to leave, when his phone rang. He turned from me for a few seconds, and I helped myself.

I mean, where else was I going to secure a weapon? He's lucky I didn't steal his gun. I wanted to, but he surely would have noticed that missing. A knife, not so much, at least not right away.

From what I hope is a safe distance, I follow the second, fingering my own weapon the whole time. I'm not convinced I can defend myself with it, but if I have to, I'll sure as hell try.

That's all I *can* do.

We turn down a corner and approach a heavy wooden door. Before we reach it, the second stops and turns to me.

I wrap my fingers around the handle of my knife and widen my stance just like my instructor showed me.

"You know, lady, you aren't worth all this bother. The *Pakhan* is wasting his time with you."

Breathe…

"Guess it's a good thing you're not in charge then, isn't it?" I quip. "And from what I know, you never *will be* in charge."

If there's one thing I've learned, it's that these men have outsized egos. The problem with that, for them, is they are easy targets for insults.

And the one I just hurled at the creep in front of me hit just the way I wanted it to.

He presses his lips together, and his face gets red, like he's holding his breath. "Women are for men's pleasure. But I am sure no man enjoys himself with an American whore like you."

He pulls open big the door, standing behind it as he holds it for me. In a flash of what I can only call brilliance, I pretend to trip, falling against the door and pushing it into his face.

Hard.

"Ahhhrrrrgggg, you bitch!" he screams, his hand flying to his nose.

Which is now dripping blood.

Oops.

"Oh my gosh, Mister Second Man, I'm so sorry. Do you need a tissue?" I ask with all the fake concern I can muster.

While he growls, he looks over my shoulder. I follow his gaze and find the *Pakhan* sitting at a large table, watching the commotion.

And as soon as I turn back to the second, I see him winding up his arm, poised to strike me.

"*Stop*!"

The *Pakhan* is on his feet, pointing.

Holy shit. I didn't count on being belted across the face by this cretin.

"You can leave now," the *Pakhan* barks at him.

Blood drips into the second's hand, and I have to say it's the most beautiful sight I've seen in I don't know how long.

I jump out of the way as he leaves. "Sorry about that. Really. And I'm all out of tissues, darnit."

The second glowers, causing me to step back further, out of his reach. "That was no accident, lady."

"Maybe you'd like to tell the *Pakhan* what you said to me just before we entered the office? Hmmm? Something about being a… whore, I think it was?" I taunt.

I'm pushing it. I know it. And I don't care.

He stands there, silent.

Yup. Just what I thought.

He can put a woman down but when it comes to owning up to it, he's a big pussy.

Loser.

He slowly pulls the door closed.

I wave goodbye to him. "See ya!"

CHAPTER THIRTEEN

Charleigh

"Miss Gates, is it?" the *Pakhan* asks, getting right down to business.

"Yes," I say politely, waiting for an invitation to sit.

Which I do, as soon as he gestures to the chair opposite him.

His office is kind of on the shabby side, surprising me, but I guess not all criminals care about fancy surroundings. Fluorescent lights glare overhead, the carpet is worn, and the huge conference table we are seated at is scratched and chipped. In another setting, its shabby look might be charming. But in a room that smells like a combination of dust and cigars, pretty much nothing is going to look nice.

Without waiting, I dive into telling the *Pakhan* everything that happened the day Dimitri nabbed me. I include more background than he probably wants about my family, as well as the low-down on the trouble my sister always gets herself into. Without interruption, he listens and nods.

He probably doesn't speak to many 'civilians,' as the guys call me. I wonder if my relatively normal life seems as unusual to him as his does to me.

I round up my speech like I'm making the case in debate club or something. "You see, the man attacked and almost killed me to make a point to the Alekseev brothers. It had nothing to do with me, per se. I was just an easy target, someone who's important to the guys."

The *Pakhan's* eyebrows rise. "Important? You're important to the Alekseevs?" he asks.

Really? Is he fucking with me? Because if he is, I don't think he's very funny.

I shrug. "You could say we're… friends."

A smile grows across the *Pakhan*'s face, revealing stained and missing teeth. I do my best to hide my revulsion as a whiff of his breath floats across the table, stinging my nostrils.

After studying me for a moment, he leans onto the table, interlacing his fingers. "Miss Gates, I have sympathy for your situation, and I thank you for sharing your perspective with me."

Is he kidding? That wasn't my *perspective,* it was facts. All facts.

Has this whole thing just been an anxiety-inducing waste of time?

Fuck these people. All of them.

I start to stand, but the *Pakhan* waves me back down. I obey, because what the hell else can I do?

"I will have Dimitri Yegorov compensate you for your trouble."

Huh?

"I… I don't think I understand," I say slowly.

"He will make restitution. To you and the Alekseevs," he says, like our conversation is over.

Not so fast.

"Um, sir, I did not come here for money. I don't want Dimitri's money."

He is perplexed. "Excuse me? Miss Gates, that is my decision—"

I cut him off. Probably not the smartest thing I've ever done. "I refuse to be monetarily compensated," I say, my chin up.

His eyes narrow and his head shifts back on his neck, like he's never had anyone, much less a woman, disagree with him.

Which is probably true.

"What is it you want, then?" he asks, amused.

Asshole.

I shrug. "It's pretty simple. I want blood."

His eyes widen, and he stifles a laugh. "Blood?" he says, smiling. "Miss Gates, do I need to remind you that Dimitri is worth more to this organization than you are?"

And there we have it. I'll never be worth as much as a man in this world.

I grip the arms of my chair and repeat in my head the guys' lecture on keeping my cool.

I will not lose my shit, I will not lose my shit...

I am not ready to give up. "How is Dimitri of value to anyone? All I hear about is what a drain he is," I say calmly.

So far, so good. I'm under control. All is right with the world. We're just discussing whether someone has the right to live or die. I'm pushing my luck but carefully. Very carefully.

The *Pakhan* drums his fingers, clearly tiring of me. "What you don't know, Miss Gates, is that Dimitri's father was an honorable man. That sort of respect is afforded to family members in our world. Even though his father is no longer with us, Dimitri is protected, to a degree. Additionally, he runs several businesses—"

"I don't care," I say, finally snapping. It was inevitable. "I'll kill him myself. Try and stop me."

I get to my feet. The *Pakhan* might not be done with our conversation, but I sure am. What a waste of fucking time.

He sighs. "Very well, Miss Gates. You have been warned. We have our ways of doing things, and I suggest you try to understand that. You can leave now. Please send in the Alekseev brothers," he says, waving me out the door.

"But—" I start to say.

"Miss Gates, I am a patient man. It would do you some good to learn patience, yourself. Now listen to me carefully." He approaches me, shaking a finger in my face.

Oh shit. I've done it now.

"I'm not used to women speaking to me the way you do. I know times are different, and that this is the way of the world now. Women say what is on their minds. They disagree. They ask for what they want. I'm not so old I don't see that. I don't like it, but I suppose I have to get used to it. Accept the new ways. After all, the world is always changing, is it not?" he asks, raising his hands.

Maybe he's more evolved than I thought.

He moves closer still, and in a swift movement,

too fast for me to move, he grabs the hair at the back of my head and yanks sideways.

"Wait—" I cry, stumbling in my uncomfortable position and high heels, wondering if I'm going down, and whether this man intends to hurt me and how badly.

"I will not accept disrespect from you, young lady."

He tugs my hair, pulling me into a torturous sideways position.

"Please," I beg, "I didn't mean—"

"You meant every word you said, Miss Gates. Every word. I am no fool. I suggest you go back home and think about what I told you."

With a final tug, he lets go. I straighten up and run for the door, wondering how close I was to losing my life.

The second waits just outside the Pakhan's office, and when I appear, walks ahead of me down the hall. Because I apparently haven't learned my lesson yet about following these strange men's rules, I rush past him, dying to get to the guys. When I fly into the room where they're waiting, they jump to their feet.

"What the hell?" Kir asks at my out of breath, disheveled appearance.

I point at the door I just passed through with the second close on my heels, as if I could actually get away from him in this rabbit warren of hallways and offices. "Guys. He wants to see you," I say. "The *Pakhan* wants to see the three of you."

As I say this, I realize that means I'll be left alone with the second. I don't know for how long, but to be honest, one second is more time than I want to spend with him.

"I'll stay here with the lady," he grouses. "End of the hall," he says, opening the door for the brothers.

"Don't worry, we know the way," Vadik says.

And now I'm alone with the creep who eyes me like he'd love to keep me and eat me for dinner.

"Hey," I say cheerfully, "your nose stopped bleeding."

Talk about poking a bear.

He lunges at me and grabs my neck. But I'm fast too, and my stiletto knife is immediately against his crotch. I would love to use it. I really would.

I could take his dick or his balls. Or both.

And he realizes that.

His hands drop from my neck, and I back away, keeping the knife visible. He needs to remember I'm not afraid of him. Or at least believe that I'm not.

"You know," I say, "I've learned the hard way to go nowhere without protection. I never used to, but after being beaten nearly to death, well, what choice does a girl have? I gotta stick up for myself, know what I mean? The guys say I'm not ready for a gun *yet,* so I came across this nice little stiletto knife. I'm dying to use it. I really am. Do you think I'll get the chance to?" I ask with a sad pout.

Across the room, he paces like a caged animal, glaring at me in the disbelief that he was just bested by a woman.

I sigh. "I was hoping to try it out, maybe on you. But as long as you stay on the other side of the room, far away from me until the guys return, I won't. And yeah, I know you have a gun and can put a bullet in my head anytime you want. But I also know you'll end up with a bullet in your own head, as will every member of your family, if you do that."

Good boy.

CHAPTER FOURTEEN

Niko

"Gentlemen, like I told your woman, you will take no action without my approval."

The *Pakhan* glowers at my brothers and me. The man does not look happy and I'm pretty sure I know why. I'll get to the bottom of it later, but I'd bet all the money I have that Charleigh stood up to him in a way we warned her not to. Sure, her pride and grievances against Dimitri are completely legit, but there is a time and a place to confront a man like the *Pakhan*. Charleigh did not choose her opportunities wisely and because we weren't in the room with her, there wasn't a damn thing we could do about it.

Not really a surprise, when it comes down to it. She's not the kind of woman to let someone run her over.

But the stern expression the *Pakhan* is wearing today for my brothers and me is not something I've seen before.

I've known this man for as long as I can remember. Our father went way back with him, all the way to their Russia days. Their mutual respect and long-standing relationship have meant an open-door policy for my brothers and me, even after Papa was gone. Regardless of the topic, our interactions are always friendly, even when we're politely disagreeing with each other.

Today is different, though.

Today, the *Pakhan* is speaking as if we're strangers undertaking an unpleasant negotiation, which I suppose we are. He's taking no chances on us misunderstanding—or 'mishearing'—his clear directive. The days of the man pretending to hide a quarter behind the ear of ten-year-old me, while Papa proudly patted me on the head, are a universe away.

No, today I am looking at an altogether different man, one who has multiple interests to protect, even if that means letting people like Charleigh get hurt.

I don't like this version of the *Pakhan*, and the more he insists we follow his lead, the less I like him. I want restitution for our girl, possibly even more than she does, and it's almost impossible not to see him as an obstacle.

We know that as long as Dimitri Yegorov walks this earth, Charleigh won't have a peaceful night's sleep. Not only is she forever looking over her shoulder, her rage is unmistakable. It's written across her face and evident in the way she walks. It's even affected the way she speaks.

Like my brothers, I want to put all this to rest for the sake of Charleigh, and also get back to our day-to-day business. Dimitri has been nothing but a pox on all our lives, really, for as long I can remember, and it's well past time for him to get his due.

How my brothers have restrained themselves from taking him out for what he did to our parents is beyond me. They have less patience than I do, their actions far less muted.

But we may be getting closer to our revenge if what Charleigh says about a 'secret room' in Dimitri's house is true. It's quite possible she imagined it. The beating she took was a serious one, and her memory is not the most trustworthy witness. But if that room exists and has evidence linking Dimitri to my parents' death, this case will be fucking closed.

No more 'being patient,' as the *Pakhan* puts it. No more bullshit payment of reparations meant to smooth over bad feelings. In the old days, in Papa's time, it might have been enough to send an injured party away with a bag full of cash. But that doesn't work anymore, and especially not with someone like Charleigh.

Which I'm sure the *Pakhan* picked up on, and which has put him in such an irritable mood. Undoubtedly, he thought he could pat Charleigh on the head, pay her off, and send her away like a good girl.

He doesn't know her like we do.

She may not have been around the block like the rest of us in the syndicate, but she has enough self-respect to ask for what she wants, and not to back down when she's refused at her first appeal.

Hands folded in front of him, Vadik takes a deep breath. The only way I know he's losing his patience is his lightly tapping foot, which the *Pakhan* fortunately can't see or hear.

"Sir," my brother starts, "I am not sure what further evidence is needed to show that Dimitri Yegorov deserves a punishment considerably more harsh than paying off Charleigh for her trouble."

The *Pakhan*'s head snaps back on its axis, screaming loud and clear that he is not having it, not having the Alekseev brothers not only question his decision, but continue to press the point.

That's too fucking bad. If he goes ballistic on us and pulls out a gun and shoots us dead, well, at least we'll know we went down trying to do the right thing for Charleigh.

Holy shit. I'd risk my life for her. I hadn't realized that until now.

Fuck, am I in trouble. At least I'm not alone. I look at my brothers, doing all they can to contain their frustration with this stubborn old man. I know we're of the same mind.

"I think you are aware that a woman in our employ was recently killed driving Niko's car," Kir says.

The *Pakhan* nods. Of course he knows. He knows all the shit that goes on.

"The truck driver who hit her, making the wreck and explosion look like an accident, was the same man who crashed into Clara and me several years ago, killing Clara. I have no doubt he was on Dimitri's payroll, then and now," Kir says.

"Where is this man now?"

"Dead."

Of course he's dead. As soon as Kir made the connection, that he was the big rig driver in both 'accidents,' it was all over for him. We took him to one of our warehouses and used everything at our disposal to 'encourage' him to tell us who was paying him. When it became clear he was not going to rat, we put an end to his miserable life.

Actually, his life would have come to an end even if he did confess who was behind his actions, but because he remained so tightlipped—probably the result of threats against his family and such—Kir made sure his demise was a pretty fucking unpleasant one. My brother has always had a bit of a flair for the dramatic. He stuck a small but sharp stiletto knife into the side of the man's neck, an injury severe enough to cause death, but not severe enough to make it happen quickly.

I don't know how long it took for the man to bleed out. I didn't stick around to watch.

Did he finally get revenge for the loss of his love, Clara? Not a chance.

The *Pakhan* drums his fingers on his desk. "Very well. I have heard you men make your case. It's a solid one, I'll give you that. But Dimitri will not be confronted. Not yet. He brings a lot of money into the faction, and I can't ignore that."

Fuck all. It comes down to money. It always does.

How much more does this fucker need? He could wipe his ass with gold toilet paper if he wanted.

But maybe there's a method to his madness, as Papa used to say. I remember his words.

Be quiet and observe, boy. A man's words don't always mean what you think they do.

I repeat Papa's appeal to myself, wanting to trust the *Pakhan*. My brothers are not nearly as introspective, and brim with anger and frustration. They are offended at what they see as the *Pakhan*'s dismissal of them, with Kir's mouth turned into a thin line and Vadik's eyes narrowed.

I'd be offended too, if I didn't have a hunch the man isn't saying everything that's on his mind. Like the *Pakhan,* I want to tell my brothers to be patient. Only they won't listen to me, just like they won't listen to him. They're not ready.

The *Pakhan* gets to his feet, signaling the end of the meeting. I'm eager for it to wrap up too. There's nothing more to accomplish today except talking around each other in circles, which is not a good use of anyone's time and is likely to push the *Pakhan* over the edge. Pissing him off is *not* more likely to get him to do what we want, but it *is* likely to get our asses kicked out of his office, possibly permanently.

I am also very happy this meeting's coming to a close because we had to leave Charleigh alone with the *Pakhan*'s second—never a good option. I've seen how his piggy little eyes run over her body, and it sickens me. He will never touch her. He won't even get close to her.

I race down the hall after the *Pakhan's* dismissal and finally burst into the room where they wait for us. Charleigh sits peacefully across the room, reading a book in her Kindle app. She looks relaxed and when we enter the room, her expression remains the same, like she's neither happy nor unhappy to see us.

That's what I miss. Charleigh's face used to light up when she saw us. I haven't seen her do that in way too long. If she gets her revenge against Dimitri, will her demeanor change?

Fuck, I hope so.

CHAPTER FIFTEEN

Niko

"Looks like you warmed the old man up for us really well, baby," Kir says with a twinkle in his eye. "You left him in a great mood."

He knows better than to expect differently. Just like Vadik and I do. But he has to get a smart-assed remark out of his system.

Gazing out the car window, she shrugs while flicking the ends of her hair. "I suppose I did. The old fucker didn't listen, though. No surprise there. He just wants Dimitri to give me a bunch of money and then send me on my way." She turns toward my brothers and me, all seated in the back of our limo, and the hatred in her eyes hits me.

Have we lost our girl forever?

She continues with a vehemence. "He doesn't care what Dimitri did to me. He doesn't care at all, which means if the man wants to do it again he can, and even worse, he knows he can get away with it. He's given carte blanche to all men to do whatever the hell they want to women, with the only consequence being writing them a check to shut them up."

I don't voice my suspicion that maybe the *Pakhan* is not blowing us off quite the way Charleigh and everyone thinks. They won't hear it right now, and I'm in no mood to argue, which would be the likely result.

Charleigh settles into her seat and shimmies her shoulders. "Hey. I pulled a knife on the *Pakhan*'s second."

My head whips in her direction at the same time as my brothers'.

Jesus, this woman.

"Charleigh, you're starting to sound like your little sister, with how out of control you are," Vadik says.

I can't tell if he's serious or just chiding her. It doesn't really matter, though. What he's saying is true.

"What the fuck, Charleigh?" Kir asks, frowning.

She reaches into her pocket and pulls out a small

knife, smugly showing it off like a kid in show-and-tell.

"Where the hell did you get that?" he asks.

She twirls it around between her fingers, admiring it. "I *borrowed* it from my self-defense instructor."

"Oh for Christ's sake," Vadik says. "And how did you come to pull a knife on the second. Did he do something to you?"

She presses her lips together, pausing. "You know that bloody nose he had? Well, when we were going into the *Pakhan*'s office, I *accidentally* pushed the door into his face."

Kir busts out laughing, but when he notices the serious look on Vadik's and my faces, he reins it in.

"And then what?" I ask.

"As you can imagine, he was kind of mad. Then the *Pakhan* made him leave, which made him even more mad. When I got back to the waiting room and you guys left, I pointed out that the bleeding had stopped."

Kir nods, still trying not to laugh. "Okay, so you were antagonizing the bastard. Not hard to do with a big-headed brute like him. But when did you pull the knife?"

"I guess I pissed him off," she says with false innocence, "so he lunged at me. I pulled the knife and held it at his crotch." She demonstrates with pride.

I'd be lying if I didn't admit to feeling a bit of pride, myself. Not a smart move on her part, but good for her for the excellent effort. Still, she could have ended up dead. And like she has observed, the penalty wouldn't be much at all, since she's 'just' a woman.

"Jesus Christ," Vadik says, rubbing his bald head.

Charleigh nods proudly. "As you might imagine, that got him to back right off."

She drops the knife back into her pocket before one of us can confiscate it.

I could tell her that her little knife might have slowed the second, but it wouldn't have stopped him from snapping her neck. I could tell her she's not the kind of badass she thinks she is, and that she needs to watch herself. Or, I could tell her to hand over the goddamn knife before she hurts herself.

But I don't. I like how she stuck up for herself, no matter how clumsily she did it.

I change the subject. "The *Pakhan* said Dimitri will be compensating you. I know that was hard for you to hear, but that's typical in our world. What's *not* typical is a woman seeking her own revenge. Keep in mind you're bucking the trend here. And when you do something like that, you have to step carefully."

She studies me as I speak, finally listening.

"I know you don't want money." I look at my brothers and decide to share my thoughts. Fuck anyone who doesn't like it. "That's a temporary fix. I know it is. We'll see more action on the *Pakhan*'s part at some point. When, I don't know, but we will."

She sighs impatiently. "Really? Is that what you think?"

Vadik throws me a warning look. I know he doesn't want me getting her hopes up, but he can fuck right off.

I know I'm right.

"You'll get your revenge, darlin'," I say. "We all will, for all the wrongs that bastard has visited on us. You've got to believe that, Charleigh."

Her eyes fill with tears and her voice cracks. "I hope you're right, Niko, because right now I hate myself. I hate being in my skin. It's like a thousand bugs are running over me all the time, taking tiny, painful bites of me, and soon there won't be anything left."

The tears begin to flow, and she reaches for my hand. "Please help me, Niko. I can't live like this. It hurts too much and… sometimes I'm afraid I'll do something crazy. I need to hang on for my sister. She has no one. No one cares about her but me, Niko," she says, dissolving into the sobs I expect she's been holding onto for too long.

I pull her to me. "I promise you, baby. I promise we'll get this all taken care of. You'll never forget what happened, but it won't rule your life like it does now. Trust me."

CHAPTER SIXTEEN

Charleigh

I bunch up the bottom of my nightgown so it doesn't drag, and walk through the compound's wet grass, watered by the evening dew.

When I was a kid, I hated grass sticking to my feet and between my toes, but something about it tonight is comforting. Cool. Refreshing. It makes me feel like I can breathe, like I've left a room full of smokers where I thought I might choke to death.

An apt description of my life, where every breath seems a struggle.

I wander through the pitch-dark property, which I know well enough by now to avoid major obstacles like trees and such. I figure security is watching me, not that it makes me feel much better. The constant alert of always looking over my shoulder has my stomach in knots. I can't eat, and unless I take one of the sleeping pills prescribed by the Alekseev's doctor, I can't sleep, either.

Hell, I can't even focus long enough to read, nor sit long enough to watch a movie on TV. The only thing I can do is walk the property. Without this, I'd lose my mind.

I have to admit, there is something magical about walking outside after dark. The birds are quieter, the air smells clean, and the breeze tickles my skin. I need to hold on to this feeling, figure out a way to carry it with me to maybe get rid of some of the rotten that's eating me from the inside out.

Which was not made better by my meeting with the *Pakhan*. Did I really think he'd listen to me, a woman? How could I be so naïve?

Actually, I've been naïve about a lot of things, not least of which was running over to the arcade with Frank that day, thinking I could whisk my sister away, after which life would be grand.

I've made mistake after mistake, like encouraging Stacey to take Niko's car. It should have been me who blew up in it that day. It was *supposed* to be me.

But if I died instead of Stacey, what would have happened to Evie? Would she have gone back to my father? Would the guys have taken care of her?

Maybe, maybe not.

Which is why I'm grateful I'm here. My days may be full of nightmares that rival those that I have at night, but at least I'm here for her. I want to help her have the life I haven't.

I glance up at the big house and through the window of Evie's room, see light flickering off the walls. I said goodnight to her an hour ago. While she's not attending school per se, I am trying to keep her on the same schedule she had before so that when she goes back, it will be a seamless transition.

But the light in her room tells me she's playing video games on her computer, something she must have picked up during her brief time with the awful Arseny.

Oh, that I could wring that fucker's neck. I hate him more than Dimitri, if that's possible. Sure, he set me up, which is bad enough, but that he used my sister to do it is a step too far. He will pay, just like his uncle. I don't know when or how, just that they *will* pay. The opportunity will present itself. I know it will.

And it won't revolve around anyone giving me a bag of cash to send me on my way. All the money in the world won't keep me safe from Dimitri. Only his death will.

And that stupid 'second' of the *Pakhan*'s. First,

who would ever want to be referred to as a 'second,' and next, how did a big lout get a job like that, anyway? Actually, I know the answer, at least I can guess at it. He's related to somebody the *Pakhan* knows. It's got to be something simple like that.

That's how most everything in this world works. Who you know. Who you're related to. Who your father did deals with.

Hell, family obligations are the only reason the Alekseevs have kept that awful Dominika around.

"Charleigh. Charleigh," a soft voice whispers, startling me, but only for a moment.

It's Niko, keeping his voice low as if disturbing the peacefulness of the night would scare it away.

The little light there is in the night sky reflects his blond hair, making it easy to seek him out in the dark. As he walks toward me, his feet squeak in the wet grass, and I realize he must be barefoot like me.

It's funny to think someone from a big organized crime family actually walks barefoot on wet grass. It just seems so incongruous for someone who buys and sells illegal firearms and other weapons, and carries a gun every time he leaves the house.

So bizarre. But what about my life isn't bizarre these days?

I like to imagine what each of the guys would

have become had they been from 'normal' families, where they could choose their own professions.

Vadik would have been the CEO of some huge, successful corporation. He'd tell people what to do all day long and when they didn't, he'd fire them without hesitation. People would bow and scrape before him in appreciation of his vast knowledge and expertise. He'd travel the world in a private jet, meeting with all manner of business and world leaders, and they'd listen to everything he had to say.

Kir is easy. His passion is so clearly cooking that he'd have become a chef. Maybe have his own Michelin-starred restaurant, be on all the cooking magazine covers, and even have a show like some top chefs do. When someone in the kitchen messed up, he'd scream at them just like the chefs on TV do, but it would be for the best, to make his assistants better at their work. They'd look back on their days of working with him and admit that while it was difficult, they'd never learned so much in such a short period of time.

Niko is a little harder. He's a ladies' man, no doubt, but part of what makes him one is also what gives him his irresistible appeal. What woman doesn't love a strong, take-charge man who can also talk about feelings and wipe away tears? Maybe Niko would have been a doctor. A kindly but sexy doctor. Or a politician. A stately senator, known for bringing together people with disparate interests and concocting a solution that makes everyone walk away happy. He'd be mentioned in history books for years to come, there would be statues of him in great parks, and his name would be spoken with hushed awe and respect.

Instead, life dealt these guys a hand that's just about as limiting as what I was given. Sure, they have a lot more money, but are they really free? Do they have the freedom I so desperately wanted when I was studying for my bookkeeping certificate?

Seems we're all birds in a gilded cage.

"Whatcha doing out here?" Niko asks, slinging an arm around my shoulders.

I'm not cold, but I snuggle into his warmth anyway. When I do, I get a whiff of his scent, which I can only describe as clean and manly, as if the soap he uses is lightly scented with lime.

In another lifetime…

No. I can't think like that.

This is my life. And it's a fucked-up mess.

But Niko's touch gives me an idea, something that's become a fallback of sorts when I want my mind and body to take a vacation to someplace I can't actually go.

Without a word, I take his hand and lead him to a

bench in the garden under a huge old oak, and with my hands on his shoulders, direct him to sit down. I pull up my nightie and straddle him with a knee on either side of his hips. He's looking up at me, and while I can't really make out his expression in the dark, I find he's smiling slightly when I run a finger over his lips.

His beautiful lips, the ones that crook into a half-smile that brings me—and probably all of womanhood—to our knees.

The man has no idea.

As soon as I'm hovering over him, his hands are between my legs, exploring, looking for a sign that will reveal what I want.

Not that there's any doubt.

When I grind into his palm, he runs his fingers between my lips before zeroing in on my clit. I moan lightly and without a word, he slides his sweatpants below his hips. After a couple strokes of his hard cock, he directs himself toward my opening.

I bury my head into the crook of his shoulder and lower myself onto him, instantly transporting myself away from the deviant life that's sucked me into its clutches, and toward a sort of nirvana, however temporary, where suffering either disappears or never actually existed to begin with.

I raise and lower myself on him and the only

sound is our breath and the breeze in the oak tree above us, and I'm floating through the headiness of my approaching orgasm. In a moment of lucidity, I wish life could be like this all the time, all day and night where mothers don't die, fathers don't gamble, and little sisters are happy.

CHAPTER SEVENTEEN

CHARLEIGH

"I love you."

I am jerked out of my post-orgasmic bliss by the whisper of a man in my ear, leaving me irritated like when someone wakes you up and you'd rather keep sleeping. I grimace, forcing my eyes open and remember I'm on top of Niko, who's still inside me. He's brushing the hair out of my face, and if it wasn't dark I'd probably see him looking intently at me, waiting for an equally romantic response.

But if it wasn't night and I could see him, my response would be the same as it is right now, and that's no response. I can't respond to a gesture like that, no matter how kindly it's intended.

I just can't.

An itchy restlessness creeps over me and I want

to run, as if that will get me away from it and my distressing feelings.

I silently uncouple myself from Niko and in a panic, am not sure what to do.

"I've told you before," he says.

"Hmmm? Told me what?" I ask, stalling.

Oh my God. I've got to get out of here before I fall into a full-blown anxiety attack. My heart is already pounding in my chest. I'm on the verge of tears. And I really don't know why.

"When you were unconscious. After the attack. I told you then."

I *could* tell him how I feel about him. I *should* tell him. But the words won't come. I can't give that much of myself away when I am barely hanging on.

So I bolt.

I jump off him and run toward the house, my nightgown gathered in front of me in a fist. The grass has gotten wetter than when I first came outside, and in my haste, it behaves like ice, and I wipe out, landing flat on my chest, my hands in front to soften the fall. They don't help.

I catch my breath and scramble to continue my escape, a little more carefully this time, until I reach the house. Praying I can slip up the stairs to my room without attracting any attention, Vadik and Kir, having a drink in the library, see me first.

I'm a sight in my wild state. There will be questions.

"Hey. What's going on out there?" Vadik asks.

I approach the doorway and look down at myself. I've got dirt on my feet and hands and wet grass stains covering the front of my nightie, making it more sheer than it already is.

"Come in here," Kir says, gesturing with his head. "What the hell is going on?"

I open my mouth to speak a couple times before I have any words. "I... we... I was just outside. I, um, slipped." I take a seat at the very end of the crackly leather sofa, closest to the door.

Just in case I need to bolt.

Kir tilts his head like he's not sure he believes me. "And... why are you out of breath? Were you running?"

I nod.

They wait for me to say more.

Shit.

"Yeah. Yes. I was running."

Vadik frowns at me. "Running from what?"

"Well, I was... with Niko. And then I ran away."

I do not want to talk about this. I do not.

The brothers look at each other. "And why would you run away from Niko?" Kir asks.

The panic that caused me to run in the first place

is thrumming in my chest again, threatening to take away my breath, or make me cry, or both, and all I want is to escape this feeling but the fucking thing follows me around like a possessed demon more often than not these days.

Maybe I'm the one who's possessed. Maybe I'm the demon.

"He told me he loved me," I say in a barely decipherable voice, staring at my dirty, twisting fingers.

"Okay," Kir says. "Is that a bad thing?"

I don't answer. I can't. Because I don't know.

I finally look at the guys and I see it, that what I was running from is also right here in this room, as if it followed me. I don't want it, I don't need it. I won't have it.

Fuck all.

Vadik sets his drink aside and leans forward in his chair.

I hold my breath because I'm pretty sure I know what's coming.

"Can you… love Niko? Can you love *us*?" he asks quietly.

Bam.

Words I never thought I'd hear come out of Vadik's mouth. The vulnerability makes me want to run to him, to comfort him, and to protect him. On one hand, I am honored… and yet I also feel like a caged animal.

Desperate for escape.

"I… well…" I sputter.

"We want you to love us. If you can. If you can't, well, that's fine too."

My head spins and the pretty books on the library walls melt together in a jumble of leather bindings and gold lettering. Please just let me pass out. The guys will put me to bed and this excruciating conversation will be forgotten.

But I don't pass out, dammit, and therefore I must respond. After all, it's the right thing to do even if I am being a chicken shit. The risk Vadik took in telling me this warrants that much respect.

"I… am honored. So honored," I whisper. "I want to tell you the same, I do. But right now, I can't. I care about you, all of you," I say, finally meeting their gazes. "I know that much."

They nod, their faces covered in understanding, which makes me hate myself more. Why can't they get angry with me? Lash out? It would make things so much easier.

That's when Niko joins us, and I'd give my life to make the pain in his eyes go away. He doesn't deserve the hurt he's wearing right now, all caused by me.

"I need time," I finally say.

It's not much, but those three words sum things up.

I know they're mystified, that I can have sex without abandon, yet when it comes time for emotional intimacy, I'm completely checked out. There was a time in my life when, on the receiving end of the same, I would be puzzled too. Now that I'm on the other side, I get it. If you're not ready, you're not ready.

Can't force a round peg in a square hole and all that.

I want to go to Niko. But that's not going to happen.

So I run.

It hurts, everything hurts, my limbs, my head, even my organs, and something causes the skin on my stomach to burn. It's strange, as if a pattern is being etched, but I can't lift my head to take a look, and in fact can't move at all, not one bit.

"Owwwww," I moan.

The pain ceases, then intensifies, then ceases again and I don't understand how this can be. This is not how things work, this is not how anything works, and I'm confused and just want to be left alone so I can go back to sleep.

"Charleigh," a voice calls, a voice that's not in the room where they're hurting me. "Charleigh," it repeats.

I force my eyes open and find Niko standing over me, not touching me, but gently trying to prod me out of my nightmare so as not to scare me too much.

"Wh... what?" I mumble.

"You were thrashing and moaning. I came to check on you," he says.

I push up on my elbows and realize I'm in my room in the big house, and no one is hurting me anymore.

I take a deep breath. The nightmares are getting old. Really old. "Thank you, Niko. I appreciate it."

He settles into the easy chair next to my bed, and I reach for his hand, scary as it is. It's so strange that I'd rather have full on sex than touch this man's fingers with my own, but I need comfort right now, and God knows Niko deserves some too.

I've been awful. And I feel so badly.

"Why don't you get up? We'll get out of the house," he suggests. "Go to the club."

Yeah. That works. A change in scenery might help.

Forty-five minutes later I'm cleaned up, having

blown out my hair, put on makeup, and dressed in some of the nice clothes the guys filled my closet with. If I can't pretend to be back to normal, at least I can look like it on the outside.

But when we reach the top floor and exit the club's elevator, any attempt at normalcy on my part flies right out the window. I begin to shake and sweat because none other than the *Pakhan*'s second is at the end of the hallway, turning into Vadik's office.

And I don't have my knife.

"Wh… what's he doing here?" I ask, grabbing Niko's sleeve.

He takes a deep breath. "Probably dropping off the 'compensation' the *Pakhan* offered you. Look, I know this is not what you want, but play along at least for now."

I nod at Niko and, holding my head up, march right for Vadik's office.

"Morning, Charleigh," Vadik says when I enter.

The second says nothing, and I don't even look at him.

"Morning, Vadik," I answer.

I stand next to him while the two are chatting, a large briefcase on the desk between them, and my rage is back like a virulent disease, the kind that only fools you into believing it's gone. It nibbles at my sensibilities like a hungry piranha, and I can feel myself losing my shit as creepy-crawlies make their way up my arms and then, because my brain isn't working, my body takes over. I reach down and pull off one of my shoes and, raising it above my head, bring the stiletto heel right down on the back of the second's hand, shattering bones and sinew and generally making a mess out of Vadik's desk with blood spray.

The room is dead quiet for a millisecond while everyone, myself included, absorbs what I've done, and as the *Pakhan*'s second comes out of his momentary shock, he hollers and screams at the bloody horror that is his impaled hand, my high-heeled shoe sticking out of it, and reaches for his gun with his good hand.

That's when Vadik and Niko jump into action. I am grabbed around the waist from behind and in spite of my flailing, am dragged out of the room by Niko, while Vadik knocks the gun from the second.

And as I'm pulled down the hall, out of reach of the injured second and his deranged but understandable rage, I realize the voice I hear screaming, asking for a gun, no, begging for a gun, is my own, and I can't turn the damn thing off.

CHAPTER EIGHTEEN

VADIK

"What in the ever-loving FUCK were you thinking?"

Charleigh looks small in the chair Niko pushed her into, and even smaller when she shrinks away from my brothers and me, all hovering over her trying to figure out just when she got so batshit crazy.

She looks from one of us to the next, without a word, because I'm pretty sure she has no goddamn answer.

"THIS is why we don't give you a gun. You are out of control. You are not only going to get yourself killed, but also, very likely, us. Jesus Christ, Charleigh, you have got to be out of your mind," I scream.

At the moment, I'm the one out of my mind, and it doesn't feel good. We have enough goddamn shit going on around here without Charleigh losing it and stabbing someone's hand with her high heel.

And it wasn't just anyone's hand she just shattered. She might not like the *Pakhan's* second—none of us do, for that matter—but she just brought a world of hurt down on all our heads. We are not pleased. Obviously, the second is not. And the *Pakhan* won't be, either.

"As long as you operate out of emotion rather than logic, not only will you not get a gun, but you will also continue to make bad decisions, decisions that drive you further away from what you really want to accomplish."

I pace the room, thinking through all the possible outcomes of Charleigh's actions and they are so numerous and grim, I dare not tell her about them.

"Is this what you want, Charleigh? Do you have a death wish? Because it sure as hell looks like it," I say, my face inches from hers.

Her eyes are wide with terror, as if she's just as surprised by her actions as the rest of us, and while that may be true, it doesn't change a thing.

Actions have consequences. Doesn't she understand this?

"And what about your sister, Charleigh? The sister who is supposedly your absolute highest priority, your biggest commitment? Because I can tell you, you are doing neither yourself, nor her, any favors."

Fuck.

I pace Niko's office, where he dragged Charleigh after she went after the second. I have to admit, there *was* satisfaction in seeing his agony, given that he's a cold and heartless bastard, but he was here at the club for a legitimate reason, and attack was entirely inappropriate.

God, I'd like to cut her loose. I never thought I'd hear myself think that, but I am seriously starting to wonder if she's worth all the trouble she brings.

"Well?" I yell. "Do you have anything to say for yourself?"

"I… I don't know what came over me," she says weakly, shaking her head in disbelief.

"No shit," I bark right back at her. "And that's exactly the problem. You have no control. You can't be trusted. And at some point, we guys won't be able to protect you from yourself. You'll find yourself dangling out there with no net, because we will have given up on your ass."

As the enormity of what she's done sinks in, she

buries her face in her hands, her shoulders shaking lightly.

"I..." she starts to mumble.

"Speak up, Charleigh. We can't hear you," Niko says in his soothing voice.

He may not look or sound as frustrated as me, but I know he is.

We are trying to help this woman, but if she keeps fucking things up, we'll have to throw in the towel.

Regardless of how we feel about her.

She's becoming a risk we can't afford to keep around.

"How... how do you guys do it?" she asks in a small voice. "How do you exist in this world, where your parents are murdered and you can't go after the man who did it? How do you wake up and go through every day with so much hate in your heart all the color has gone out of everything?"

I know what she's describing. Yeah, we know how it is when you think you'll never be able to smile again. But if you let the hate destroy you, you'll never get your revenge.

I stop my pacing and take a seat. I can't risk a migraine today. That would fuck things up worse than they already are.

"Charleigh, don't you know I suffer every day? I

mean, I can't speak for my brothers, but I'm guessing it's the same for them on some level."

I look up at Kir and Niko and they nod at what I just shared, something I've never, ever said out loud. Hey, I might be a bastard, but I feel shit like anybody else.

"Every day we get closer to the revenge we seek for our parent's death. It's not easy. My father was bigger than life. I feel like he's sitting on my shoulder every day. I put massive pressure on myself. People call me a workaholic. I feel like the man can see my every move. Sometimes I'm so angry he was murdered that I can't even see straight. But I don't let that cloud my judgement. If I fucked up, I'd never get to avenge his death."

I pull her out of the chair where she's sitting and bring her over to the sofa where I can wrap my arms around her.

Initially, she stiffens in my embrace, as if my touch stings, but a few whispered words help her gradually relax. She drops her head onto my shoulder, and my brothers leave us to go take care of the situation she caused.

It feels good that she's trusting me, and that I'm able to make her at ease. But I have to wonder, for myself, what it means for me, too.

On one hand, I want to run probably as much as

Charleigh does. But on the other, I think I am finally learning what I really want.

And that's scary as hell.

CHAPTER NINETEEN

VADIK

I take Charleigh's chin and turn it toward me. Since before she went crazy on the second's hand, I've been unable to take my eyes off her lips, perfectly shaped, colored with a light red stain that almost makes them look bruised.

When she whacked the man with her high heel, the look of satisfaction that washed over her wild face when the sound of crushing bones filled the room solidified the fact that the old Charleigh is gone. The new Charleigh has a blackened heart obsessed with revenge. She is able to fuck with abandon but has no capacity for true connection, and doesn't hesitate to stand up to men twice her size as if she has some sort of death wish.

Which she probably does.

After yesterday's conversation, when she was unable to respond to my brothers and me expressing our care for her, I told myself I'd keep my distance. I don't like the feelings I have for her. They will bring nothing but trouble for me and the Alekseev name.

But she looks so wild and insolent with her hair askew and rebellion in her eyes. She has a new strength in her. Now, if only it can be channeled for her own good.

So far, most every decision she's made has been a shitty one.

Like maiming the *Pakhan*'s second. I have half a mind to buy Charleigh a one-way plane ticket someplace very far away and tell her to disappear for the rest of her life, because that's how long she's going to be hunted now. She made her own bed and until we cut her loose, we Alekseevs have to lie in it with her. Every crazy thing she does reverberates through my brothers and me, then to our team, and down to our myriad businesses.

She's got to learn she's not living in a silo. Every action causes a reaction. Actually, multiple reactions. That's how our lives and businesses work, each component moving in time with the next like a well-oiled machine. She has to work with us or... not at all.

But I haven't given up hope. She can be tamed.

And when that wild energy is harnessed and focused, she will be more of a force to contend with than she already is.

I brush my lips against hers, and she hungrily demands more, catching the back of my neck and pulling me to her with a daunting hunger, and as much as I want to take her and help her forget her the cruelties the world has visited on her, she has a lesson to learn.

To her surprise, I push her back, and she looks at me with widened eyes, like I deprived her of something she's entitled to.

She's not entitled to anything, not a goddamn thing, and she's going to learn that right now.

"Charleigh?"

Ignoring my questions, she lunges at me, attempting to return to our kiss like her life depends on it.

I restrain her. Again.

"Listen to me, Charleigh."

"*What?*" she snaps, going for the buttons on my shirt.

"Stop it," I say gently, taking her wrists and holding them down at her sides.

She struggles to get out of my grip. "Fine. Whatever. I've had enough of this place today, with you guys selling my well-being to buy my silence. Go fuck yourself," she hisses.

Now we're getting somewhere.

She tries to get to her feet but is effectively immobilized by my holding her still.

"Get off," she growls, pulling and struggling.

"Goddammit, Charleigh, sit down and shut up!" I yell.

This catches her by surprise and puts an end to her mini tantrum. She stops resisting and looks at me with curiosity.

"You've got to start listening to me. My brothers too, until you understand how things are done around here. You might not like everything you are told but believe me, each decision we make is made with a view to a bigger picture. You will get your revenge, and when you do, I hope it's all you want and more. But until then, you are fucking things up not only for yourself but for my brothers and me. That's not gonna work."

The defiance in her eyes drains away, and she hangs her head. She's tired. I know she is. Tired of always being on alert, and tired of living with so much hate.

Her posture softens before me and I'm pretty sure I'm looking at the old Charleigh, or at least some version of her. I take her and kiss her again, and this time it's warm and intimate as opposed to greedy and demanding.

"Baby, I want you to suck my dick," I say, opening my pants.

In fact, my dick has been hard since she attacked the second, and while she never should have done that, it was hot as fucking hell.

Not that I'll tell her that.

She smiles at me knowingly and with confidence, so different from some weeks ago when she was practically afraid of a stiff cock, and didn't know any more about sucking one than a nun. I hand her a pillow, which she places under her knees.

Once situated before me, she takes me in hand and strokes me a few times, gazing at me like she's never seen my erection before. She rubs a thumb over my first drop of sticky precum and smears it around the head of my dick. With a glance at me, I nod as if to give her the go-ahead, and my cock disappears between her pretty lips, my erection cloaked by her warm, swirling tongue. I place one hand on her head and gently direct her rhythm to match my need to blow off some steam, and goddamn if she doesn't perform like a champ.

Up and down she bobs, occasionally meeting my gaze like a sweet young thing hoping for approval. But because I'm an asshole, I don't give it, I just indicate she keep going because my orgasm is more important than anything in the world at this moment.

My eruption takes her by surprise, filling her mouth until she sputters and coughs, and I swear to God, there is nothing like a beautiful woman on the end of your cock, licking it clean and enjoying every drop of your cum.

As soon as we're put back together, I figure we ought to vacate Niko's office, where we fled to get away from the second's understandably murderous rage, and return to mine. When we get there, Dominika is elbow-deep in a bucket of soapy water, scrubbing the blood off my desk—Papa's old desk—and the carpet below it.

I am so taken aback to see Dominika cleaning I nearly burst out laughing. But I'm sure she's already in a pissy mood and making it worse would be a real dick move. I just got an amazing fucking blowjob and am feeling generous, so I say nothing.

Charleigh, apparently, doesn't feel the same way.

"Yo, Dominika," she calls.

Dominika looks in Charleigh's direction and if looks could kill, my pretty girl would be laid out dead right there on the floor having taken her last breath just before she decided to antagonize the woman who must be one of the biggest bitches in history.

And for some unfathomable reason, also my father's favorite mistress.

Charleigh approaches Dominika, and I silently hope she isn't pulling any more shit today. I don't think I could handle it.

Charleigh bends real close to my desk, and points at, from where I am standing, not much of anything.

"Dominika, looks like you missed a spot."

Well, fuck me.

CHAPTER TWENTY

Charleigh

Why the hell is my sister calling me if she's just down the hall?

Unless… she isn't…

I swipe the call open. "Evie, can you just walk down to my room if you want to talk?" I start to hang up when I hear whimpering.

What the hell.

"Char, Char," she says breathlessly, "I'm not… I'm not at the compound—"

I'm going to kill her. That's it. I'm just going to kill this kid.

In the background, I hear a door shut and clothes hangers jingle. Is she in a closet?

"Char, I'm at home. Like, *our* home. Oh, Char, I'm

scared. One of my friends just called to tell me the pawn shop burned down."

What?

No.

Burned down? Like in flames?

No. God no.

"I'm on my way," I growl. "Don't move a fucking finger. Do you hear me?"

I'm silent as Kir speeds across town to what Evie refers to as 'her real home.' Actually, no one in the car makes a sound, including Vadik in the front passenger seat.

Inside the hermetically sealed thrum of Kir's very expensive Mercedes, outside noise is reduced to the extent where I suspect we can all hear my heart thumping against my chest.

Is this going to be another arcade situation? Is this a set-up, one that my foolish sister agreed to, which strangely made sense to her developing teenage brain?

Am I putting Kir and Vadik in danger the way I did Frank, not to mention myself?

Dear God, please don't let this be another trap. I just want to get my sister, drag her back to the compound, and lock her in her room until she's a legal adult. Then she can do all the bone-headed things she wants to because there will be nothing I can do about it. And hopefully at that point, I won't care anymore. I can only bring this kid along so far. If she wants to live her life like a little fool, and so far it's looking like that, it's her choice.

I can only lead her so far, and I can honestly say I'm close to throwing in the towel right now, even though the punk is still underage and is about as far from adulthood as a teenager can be.

I didn't ask, because I was afraid to, but I'm hoping Kir drives past the pawn shop so I can see if it really burned. I know we don't have time for that right now—the priority is Evie—but I just want to *know*.

The truth is, however, I am almost positive Kir is actually *avoiding* driving past the pawn shop until we get more information about what the hell is going on with it, and whether it's even safe for us to approach it.

Then there's the question of Pops. It's eerie—heartbreaking, really—how when Evie called, she became my first priority, followed by the safety of the guys when they told me they'd take me to her. Pops only crossed my mind later, much later, when it occurred to me to wonder where the hell he was. My father didn't even rank. Truth is, he doesn't deserve to, and if that's not tragic, I don't know what is.

I never thought I'd get to a point like this about my father, but then I never thought about a lot of thing things my life has turned into.

Just one freaking surprise after another.

After I mutilated the second's hand yesterday, I was shocked as hell they made Dominika clean up the mess rather than me. If that woman didn't already resent the hell out of me, she sure does now. In fact, because she's the kind of person who always needs to deliver her parting shot, as she was leaving the room, she took the time to tell me how she really feels about me.

"You're just another Alekseev whore. Wait 'til they're done with you. You'll be ruined. You'll be less than nothing," she hissed.

I sighed and picked at the manicure Evie tried to give me, already chipping and looking like crap. "You should know, Dominika. You should know."

That's when Vadik jumped to his feet, certain he was going to have to break up a cat fight. But Dominika just left, and when Vadik sat back down, his expression was part amusement, part annoyance.

Two for one. I'm getting good at that.

"Charleigh, for the rest of the day, can you just not stir up any more shit? No more hitting people, no more being a big mouth? Just for one day? Please?"

I nodded obediently, although I think we both know that, given the chance, I'd do what I did all over again. The guys can't really get too mad about that. After all, they turned me into this… whatever I am.

I had a few hours of feeling impressed with my bad self, which should have been a warning. As my mother used to say, 'pride goeth before a fall.' Just as I settled in for a good night's sleep, smug in the knowledge that I bested two of my biggest adversaries, comes the call from Evie, yanking me out of my self-important confidence, back to the shittiness of my real life.

Something always, always, has to go wrong.

Why, God? Why can't I just have a full twenty-four hours of easy living? Why does everything have to be such a freaking challenge?

God doesn't answer.

When we arrive at my father's apartment complex, we drive around a few times so the guys can assess the situation. When things seem safe, or at least as safe as they can be, Kir parks in the back of the building and we approach it, with them in the lead, guns drawn.

Like Vadik says, this will not be a repeat of what happened last time I went to fetch Evie.

I'm not as confident.

My adrenaline is running like a firehose, and my head is pounding in time to my heart. This bullshit is going to put me in an early grave, I have no doubt. A body can only take so much fight or flight before it throws in the towel, worn down like an old automotive engine driven way past its prime.

With my key, Kir opens the door to my father's apartment, ready for anything that might happen. Evie swore to me over the phone she was in there alone, but one, who knows if she's telling the truth, and two, whether someone's holding a gun to her head and telling her what to say.

Anything's possible. I've learned that the hard way.

I wait by the door while they clear the place and when they lower their guns to their sides, I rush in.

"Evie! Where are you?"

CHAPTER TWENTY-ONE

Charleigh

The apartment is musty and smells bad, faintly of urine. I'm not surprised.

A closet door bangs open and footsteps run in my direction. "Char, Char, oh my God, Char," Evie cries, throwing herself into my arms.

I want to hang onto my anger, to scold her, to let her know how pissed I am. But instead, I'm transported back, as I'm sure she is, to when she did the same in the weeks and months after we lost our mother. There was no comforting her as a six-year-old, and I'm not sure much has changed in ten years.

"Char, I was so scared. I didn't know if those men were coming for you or me."

Vadik directs the two of us, still embracing, to the sofa. I push aside some dirty laundry—why it's on the living room sofa and not in the laundry room, I can only guess—and take one of Evie's hands to get her attention.

She pulls her head out of my chest and looks at him, sniffling with a tear-stained face.

"Evie, what the hell? What the hell are you doing here?" he asks.

She rubs her nose with her sleeve. "I missed school. I missed my friends. I thought I could just live here with Pops again, and everything would go back to normal."

"You know that's not possible," I say.

She wrings her hands. "I know. I mean, I guess I know. But I don't want it to be that way. I want to go back to how things were. I don't want to live on the compound with you and the guys, and have the housekeeper tutor me. It's not normal. It's weird. And creepy."

I close my eyes and take a deep breath for patience, but before I can scold her, Kir jumps in. He's right to. First things first.

"Evie, we'll get to how you managed to leave the compound undetected later, and believe me, we will be discussing this at length. But in the meantime, how did you get here and how did you hear about the pawn shop?" he asks.

"I… I got a ride from a friend who just got her

license. I know we're not supposed to ride with kids when there are no parents in the car, but we thought it would be okay just this once. She told me there was a rumor going around at school that the pawn shop was burning down. With me in it." She bursts into tears again, I'm not sure whether more upset by the shop being gone or insulted by the kids who made up the rumor she went down with it.

"How do the kids at school know?" he asks.

He's clearly been out of school too long. One person hears something or *thinks* they hear something, and word spreads faster than wildfire.

She snuffles, and Vadik passes her a tissue he dug up somewhere in the apartment. "I think someone drove past it on the way to school. I'm not sure."

"Did they say anything about Pops?" I ask cautiously.

I've been calling him since Evie first alerted me, but no answer. Same with Victoria. In spite of my feelings for my father, a lump builds in my throat when I think about what might have happened to him.

Vadik leaves the room to make a call, which I can hear bits and pieces of. I keep Evie talking because I don't want her to hear him, but I do catch that he is sending some of his people over to the shop to investigate.

I don't say anything in front of my sister, but I know it was Dimitri. I just know it. Whether it was retaliation for what I did to the second's hand, or just a general desire to terrorize me and let the guys know they can't do anything to stop it, I don't know.

Does it really matter?

"Look, Evie," Kir says, "I get that you want to be back at school with your friends. Hopefully, someday we can make that happen. But not today. If people are after your father's shop," —he pauses before he says too much— "they may also be after you. In fact, I can pretty much guarantee they are."

Her eyes widen with fear. Are Kir's words finally sinking in?

I pull Evie to her feet. "Got get a bag and gather up as much stuff as you can. We're heading back to the compound. I'll be getting some things too."

She runs off to her room as Vadik returns. "It's definitely arson." He looks around to make sure Evie is out of earshot. "Your father didn't make it, Charleigh. I'm sorry."

I stifle a sob. As strange as it is, I wrack my brain for the last time I saw him, wondering whether I was cross with him or not.

I'm pretty sure I was.

And for all that he put me through, I still feel

shitty. If I had known his days were numbered, would I have behaved differently?

Would he have?

I gulp. "Do you… do you know if he suffered?" I ask, my voice cracking.

Vadik comes over and puts his hands on either side of my face. "I know for a fact he didn't suffer, darling. It looks like he was… shot before the fire was set."

My legs collapse under me and I fall back onto the sofa, the sofa that has been in my family all my life, where I used to watch TV with my mother, where we would sit when opening our Christmas presents, and where I would nap on the days I stayed home from school sick. For a moment, I wonder what will happen to this faded sofa, whose cushions are compressed from a lifetime of sitting and whose arms are in tatters. I look around the room. The likelihood is, it will go to the dump. Everything will go to the dump.

A lifetime of memories, taken to the dump.

How perfectly appropriate.

"C'mon, Charleigh," Vadik says, helping me to my feet. "Let's pack up some things and head back to the compound."

I nod and let him lead me toward the bedrooms,

but then stop. "I'm worried about Victoria. Did they say a woman was found in the store, by chance?"

Vadik shakes his head. "Your father was alone."

"Can we stop by Victoria's place then? On the way back to the compound?" I ask.

"Of course, darlin'," Vadik says, kissing my forehead.

"Why are you taking some of Dad's things?" Evie asks. "Did something happen to him… in the fire?"

I hate to lie, but I can't talk about Pops right now.

"We… don't know yet. But we will soon."

That seems to satisfy her, and she throws a small duffel in Kir's trunk. I notice she also has the teddy bear from her nightstand, a long-ago gift from our mother.

"We're swinging by Vic's to see if she's home, Evie. Then we'll go back to the compound."

She nods distractedly, scrolling through TikTok like a comforting security blanket.

"Hello?" I call, slowly entering Victoria's apartment after the guys clear it.

"It's so dark. And empty," Evie says, holding onto the side of my shirt.

I flick on a light and it's obvious someone has

moved out, and moved out fast. There is crap all over the place, as if Victoria went through her things and selected only the items she couldn't live without. Drawers are pulled from dressers, clothes are strewn all over, the closet is full of empty hangers, and even the pillows are missing from her unmade bed.

I guess if I was taking off, I'd take my pillow too.

I wander to the kitchen and see cabinet doors hanging open, some empty and some full, most likely because Victoria had to be selective about what she brought on her journey. There's a cold cup of tea on the counter with a tea bag still in it, as if Victoria was making herself a cup and was interrupted.

Interrupted by what? How much does she know? Is her life in danger?

A lump grows in my throat and I realize how tired I am of crying, how the grief never seems to stop coming, and how the universe just won't give me a goddamn break.

I'm tired. So tired. Of it all.

"C'mon, Charleigh. It's obvious she's not here. She left in a hurry. Okay?" Kir asks, rubbing my back.

I take one last look around at this place that's not unlike my father's—shabby but well-loved furniture, a few trinkets acquired over the years, and the sense of someone who's inhabited a place for a very long time.

She must have been scared shitless to leave the way she did.

Before we head out, I run back to her room. I want something of hers, anything, something small. I spot her fluffy bedroom slippers and pull them to my chest like they're some great treasure or something. Some people might think my choice creepy, but I am comforted by holding something so clearly Victoria's.

I have so many questions tumbling around in my head, not to mention the need to somehow break the news to Evie about our father, but I just want to get back to the compound because it's the only place where I feel a modicum of safety. The only thing that could make me feel safer, aside from Dimitri being buried six feet under, is if I could carry a weapon like the guys do. In fact, before we left to collect my sister, I ran to the gun cabinet, which was locked, of course. I've been practicing my shooting and plan to show the guys my new expertise first chance I get. If they let me.

But that's no guarantee they'll finally grant me the privilege of having a firearm. As Niko tried to explain, I might have gained the physical skills to use a gun, but I am a long way from having the emotional skills. He has a point.

But that doesn't mean I'm not impatient.

I know they want to see me more in control, more level-headed before I carry a gun, but with the rage bubbling over inside me, I am not convinced that will ever happen. And if Dimitri is behind my father's death, well, that might just push me over an edge that I'm already precariously close to.

I mean, how much does one person have to fucking take before they crack?

CHAPTER TWENTY-TWO

Kir

"Honey. I wanted to wait until we got home before I told you." Charleigh takes a deep breath and holds her younger sister's hand where they sit on the big leather sofa in the library.

I debate whether my brothers and I should leave them alone while Charleigh breaks the bad news to her sister, but figure we're in the middle of this too.

"Pops is gone, Evie."

Her face is blank at first, then she frowns, then yanks her hand from Charleigh's. "No, he's not!" she yells, jumping to her feet.

She runs for the doorway just in time for Niko to pull the doors shut, blocking her.

"Let me out!" she shouts, trying to reach around him.

But with one swift move, he has both her wrists in one of his hands and for all her struggling, she can make no progress.

So she tries to bite him. Not smart.

"Jesus, child," Niko hollers.

I can probably count on one hand the number of times I've heard my youngest brother raise his voice.

I reach into the drawer of one of our end tables, and pull out a handful of zip ties. I never thought I'd be using them on a sixteen-year-old, but I never thought we'd have one living with us, either.

Niko deftly gets Evie's hands behind her back, and before she knows it, she's restrained.

Charleigh looks upset for a moment, but then understands what we're doing is for her sister's own good.

"Go sit over there with your sister," Niko barks, pointing toward Charleigh.

Evie runs back to the sofa, and with her hands tied behind her back, buries her face in her sister's shoulder and sobs while Charleigh rubs her back.

As frustrating as this kid is, it's sad to see her lose her father. I mean, she knows nothing about what a loser he was, and unless Charleigh decides to tell her, she never will. All she knows is that he was pretty checked out after their mom died, and that he was an otherwise okay guy. Not a very hands-on father, but did Evie ever know any different?

"Wh... what happened?" she sobs.

Charleigh smooths her hair. "He was shot, honey. He died fast. He didn't suffer."

"But why?" Evie wails.

Charleigh looks at me, her expression begging for help.

"Evie, we don't know exactly what happened yet, with either the pawn shop or your dad, but we are working on it," I say.

She looks at the floor, tears streaming down her face, then narrows her eyes at my brothers and me, her face red and distorted, spit flying out of her mouth. "It never would have happened if not for *you* guys," she screams.

That's not exactly true, that we're the cause of her father's demise. The man dug his own grave, so to speak. But no need to get into that now.

"It was probably the same person who hurt you and me," Charleigh says. "That's why we must be so careful. If they knew you were at Pops's apartment, chances are they would have come after you too."

After several minutes of sobbing, Evie starts to calm, unable to wipe her tears because of her restraints. She's so pathetic and yet I'm not sure I'm ready to remove the zip ties yet.

"Fuck this. Fuck you all. Charleigh, our lives are so messed up right now. What are we going to do?"

Charleigh takes hold of her sister's chin and looks straight at her. "We are going to stay here on the compound unless we're out with the guys. We are going to listen to what they ask of us. And we're going to keep you up with your schoolwork."

"C… can you take these things off my hands now?" she asks.

I reach in my pocket for a knife and cut them clean off. I don't know if Evie is more surprised I had a knife within reach or that the ties came off so easily. "Your sister is right, Evie. You must listen. When you don't, you not only put yourself in danger but also the rest of us. What if we'd gone over there and walked into a trap, like the one you helped set for Charleigh at the arcade? We could have all been killed. Over nothing. So, please promise you won't do things like that again."

She rubs her wrists. "Sorry," she mumbles. When Charleigh nudges her, she speaks up a little. "I'm sorry. I didn't know I was making such a mess of things."

"Next time you have something on your mind, or something you're unhappy about, come tell one of us first. You can come to your sister, my brothers or me, or even Gloria. Just don't take it upon yourself to problem solve. It could get you killed," I say.

Her face is crossed with terror, which I hate to inflict on someone, but if it gets the message across to this stubborn teenager, I'm good with it.

"We're going to find out who killed your father, Evie. Mark my words," Vadik adds.

Charleigh doesn't look that torn up about her father, which is understandable. I mean, she looks sad, for sure, but she's far from broken hearted. I guess resigned would be the best way to describe her, almost as if she expected him to meet his end this way.

Niko opens the library doors and lets the housekeeper enter. "Evie, go ahead and go upstairs now with Gloria. Take a bath and watch a movie or something. Okay?"

She nods and the housekeeper puts her arm around her as she leads her away, offering her something to eat like she always does.

Satisfied all is taken care of, Charleigh leans forward and buries her face in her hands. "When is this going to stop? It's out of hand. Is Dimitri completely off his rocker?"

I hate to see our girl suffering, and it's made all the worse knowing a fucker like Dimitri is behind it. I wish I could get my hands around his neck right now. I'd enjoy slowly choking the life out of him, watching his face turn red and then purple, his eyes bulge, and his tongue spill out of his mouth.

I try not to be a gruesome fucker, but here we are.

"I'm worried about Victoria," Charleigh says.

The woman's slippers sit on the floor next to Charleigh, alongside the other things she brought from her father's apartment. It's funny Charleigh chose those, out of all the things Victoria left behind, but I get it. Slippers are personal. Intimate.

"We'll do what we can, but we don't have much to go on with her. She's kind of like a ghost. Even the first time we checked her out, before we had to confront your father, we found very little about her. Interesting person," I say.

Most people are very easy to find out about. Too easy, even if you don't have access to all the fact-finding tools my brothers and I do. Hell, we can find social security numbers, credit card numbers, you name it. Nothing is safe if we want it.

And yet, Victoria had little or no imprint. We found no bank accounts with her name, no credit cards—I don't think she even had a lease for the apartment where she lived. She probably paid her rent in cash and never made a sound, so her landlord never bothered her to sign anything. It's all very odd, but this has enabled her to slip away undetected. It's likely that unless she contacts Charleigh, she will never be heard from again.

Under the circumstances, that's a good thing. If she did eventually end up on Dimitri's radar, it's best that she not be found.

Not that that's any comfort to Charleigh.

"We'll do what we can, darlin'," Vadik adds, "but I personally think she's better off disappearing like she has. She's much safer that way."

Much safer than Charleigh and her sister, for sure.

CHAPTER TWENTY-THREE

Kir

My brothers go off to bed, leaving me hanging out with Charleigh in the library, a room I love at night. When we rebuilt from the fire that killed my parents, I wasn't sure any of the magic of the house I grew up in could be replicated. But this room, my favorite, is perfect. In the evening, when it's dark out, the room holds a sort of golden cast, perhaps because of the leather-bound books lining the wall and the dark paneled walls. I don't know crap about decorating—I leave that to the pros—but something about the place is magical, and I am psyched to be here with Charleigh, alone.

I take a seat on the sofa next to her after pouring us each a scotch and reach for her free hand. Unfortunately, she slides hers out of mine, returning hers to her lap.

Okay. No hand holding. That's cool.

"I'm sorry about your father, Charleigh. It sucks when both your parents are gone."

This I know, firsthand.

It sucks to lose anyone, but losing your parents is a special kind of pain. You've known them literally all your life, longer than anyone else in the world. And one day, they're gone. You might be an adult, but it does leave you hanging there, swinging in the wind, like a deserted little kid.

That shit never really goes away.

Charleigh shrugs one shoulder like she couldn't care less.

False bravado. I see that all the time in my business.

She sighs. "I guess it was bound to happen. The man was skating on thin ice for so long. But on the other hand, who knew Dimitri would go after him as revenge against *me*? Against *us*?"

I wouldn't put anything past him, but he has to know that every time he does something like this, the price on his head just grows and grows. He can't show his face in the light of day now, we have so many men in the field hunting him down. It can't be a pleasant way to live. Who knows, maybe he's left the country to live out the rest of his days under an assumed identity. That's what I would do if I were him.

Not that our men can't find him living under an alias. It's amazing what you can do with the right connections and enough money.

Charleigh looks at me. "Hey, did I overhear someone earlier talking about the truck driver who crashed into Stacey? Like you've seen him before or something?"

I pause. If I talk about this, I have to talk about Clara.

But the woman deserves answers.

"Yeah. The big rig driver who hit Stacey was the same truck driver who hit Clara and me a few years back. Seems neither were accidents."

She grabs her stomach. "*What*?" she whispers.

"All these years I thought it was a random accident that took Clara from me. But it was intentional, and it was intended to take *me* out. Not her. So, in the end, it's still my fault. She hadn't wanted to go out that night but I pressured her into it."

Charleigh grabs my arm. "You can't say that, Kir. Anyone could have been in the car with you."

She weaves her fingers into mine, her hand small but warm.

"It hit you hard, didn't it?" she asks quietly.

That would be an understatement.

"Do you still listen to her music?" Charleigh asks.

My head whips in her direction. "How do you know about that? Who told you?"

She sighs, rubbing her thumb over the top of my hand, her soft pale skin a contrast to my darker, weather-beaten skin.

It's funny Charleigh's asking me that question. As much as I would have preferred to keep my music-listening habits private, the truth is in recent months I have listened to Clara's recordings less and less. Not that I don't still miss her. I just have… less of a need to punish myself by playing her songs over and over.

"Niko told me you play her stuff, I think. I'm not sure, but it was a while ago. Was she a good singer?"

I wait for the stab in the heart that hits me every time I talk about her. But for some reason, this time, it doesn't come.

Instead, thinking about her feels kind of good. "She was an amazing singer. She was doing lounge acts when I met her, playing piano and singing. She'd just started making recordings, at my encouragement, when she died."

Charleigh looks at our clasped hands. "I'm so sorry. It must have been devastating."

Time to change the subject.

"What was it like for you when your mother died?" I ask.

She gives a little laugh. "Same. I'd wake up every morning looking for her. When I'd remember she was gone, I was bereft. So lost. So empty. A ten-year-old kid needs her mother. What kept me going was taking care of Evie. Like right now, she's still part of what's keeping me going."

"What else is keeping you going?" I ask, kissing her behind her ear.

Her breath comes out in a rush, like she's been holding it and finally let it go. My girl is holding on to a lot right now… and it's my job to help her plow through it so she can get back to herself and find her heart again.

If it's not already too late.

CHAPTER TWENTY-FOUR

Charleigh

"Oh c'mon, Charleigh. Don't make me do schoolwork today."

Evie flops back over in bed and tugs the comforter over her head. But I yank it right back down and in fact, pull it all the way off the bed, leaving her thrashing around in her favorite striped pajamas, which make her look like a prison inmate.

"You suck," she whines. "I'm grieving."

Really?

"Yeah, I know I suck. I also know you're grieving. So am I. But you can still learn. Now get up and get dressed. We have to head over to the school to get some of your books. I need to speak to the principal too."

She wrinkles her nose. "What are you *wearing*?"

she asks when she finally sits up in bed and looks me up and down.

I step in front of the full-length mirror on her wall and check myself out. Creamy white trousers, an off-white blouse, and a nice wide belt to pull it all together. "What? I think I look nice."

I read somewhere about wearing neutrals and that they take the guesswork out of putting together prints and other colors.

A uniform, of sorts. Works for me. It's the only way I'll get away from my usual uniform of jeans and sneakers.

Plus, they say wearing all one color makes you look like a rich lady. Not that I care about something like that. I mean, who do I see except people here on the compound?

She shrugs as she finally rolls out of bed. "I guess. But you look weird."

"I don't know what you mean," I say haughtily, checking out my ass, all nice and smooth thanks to Spanx.

Which the guys did not purchase for me. I got the housekeeper to order them for me from the internet. We're not supposed to get packages here, another security thing I guess, but the household staff seem to be allowed to.

God forbid the guys see me in my modern-day

girdle though. If it looks like any sexy time is about to go down, I have to slip out and quickly change into a thong.

I guess to Evie, I do look weird. I no longer wear the clothing that has been a uniform for me nearly all my life—jeans, Converse Chucks, T-shirts, and a hoodie, depending on how cold it is. Well, most of the time. When life gets back to normal and I can run out for coffee or something, jeans and a hoodie will have to do.

The guys have filled a closet for me—or rather, hired someone else to—loaded with silk blouses, well-fitting slacks, and cashmere sweaters. I also have a stash of shoes to choose from, mostly high heels, except for the one I used to stab a man's hand with. That pair is long gone. I'm not asking about it.

In fact, I have so many clothes now it's almost embarrassing. I'm not into waste and seriously wonder how I'll ever wear all these beautiful things. The shoes themselves are so plentiful I have a hard time choosing every time I get dressed. So, I pretty much wear the same ones, over and over.

I don't mind my new look or having a closet full of nice things. There was a time when I would have scoffed at the 'lady who lunches' look, but I don't give a shit now. I like looking nice, and the guys like it too.

Something I never thought I'd say. Not because they never *wouldn't* think I look nice, but more because I never thought I'd care about what they thought.

I tried not to, God knows. I never wanted to like anything about these guys. After all, they up-ended my life, not to mention my sister's, and are even indirectly responsible for my father losing his life.

One would think I'd be trying to get away from them as fast as possible, like I once was. But that's behind me now, and I'm not even sure I can explain why.

Well, aside from the obvious. All I have to do is set foot in public without protection, and Dimitri or some other of their enemies will scoop me right off the street and do any manner of horrible things to me.

So really, people are after me because of them, who I was forced to be with to begin with, and now I'm stuck with them because they're the only way I can stay alive.

They're the cause of my problems but also the solution.

How's that for fucked up?

But they light something up in me. Even in my darkest days, they have a way of pulling me away from the abyss, taking me to a place where things are beautiful and easy, even if it's only for a short time. It's like a drug, and I am afraid I'm becoming addicted.

If I'm not already.

Evie appears in front of me, ready for our outing, and back to her usual heavy black makeup and goth clothes in case any of her friends see her. "I don't know why I need to go," she huffs. "Can't we just send Gloria?"

"She's not our personal errand runner, Evie. We need to make an appearance at the school to show we're okay, doing well, even though Pops just died and the shop is gone. People talk and believe me, I'm sure we're the subject of a lot of speculation right now."

We pass through the kitchen so Evie can grab a bagel, and we run right into Kir, grabbing himself a cup of coffee. He looks at me out of the corner of his eye with a little smile, and I nearly melt right there.

I don't care how many people are around. I walk up to him and nuzzle my nose into his neck. It feels so normal and damn if he doesn't smell good.

"How'd you sleep. darlin'?" he asks.

I look at him coyly. "Very well, especially after… spending time with you in the library."

No, I can't hold hands with the man, but I can fuck the shit out of him. He doesn't seem to mind.

He turns from the coffee machine to face me and leans down to place a kiss on my forehead. Then he gets right next to my ear. "Good, baby, because next time I'm not going to just play with your ass, I'm going to fuck it. Hard."

Oh God. I nearly melt right there in my pretty monochromatic cream-colored outfit like the useless pile of mush he's just turned me into.

Dammit. How does he do that?

Then he pulls away from my ear. "Heading over to the school this morning, Evie? Gonna get some A's for us?" he asks.

She shrugs a shoulder and grunts.

Nice.

"Evie, answer Kir. Show him some respect. After all, you're in his house, eating his food."

She straightens up as she pulls her backpack on. "Yes, Kir," she says with exaggerated politeness. "I will be getting A's today just like I always do." She snorts.

Punk.

I exhale, counting to five, so I don't blow up on her.

Kir notices and snickers, probably glad she's not his problem. Not entirely, anyway.

"So you guys are set with the driver, right? He's taking you?" he asks.

It's more of a statement than a question. Since the attack on Stacey, they don't want me driving. I don't know how I'm safer in a limo, but if it makes them feel better, fine.

"Yup, we're all set, and in fact, he's waiting for us. C'mon, Evie," I say, taking her by the arm.

She follows along like she's all put out or something, more for dramatic effect than anything. Kir and I ignore her theatrics, and I remind myself to be patient. Just a couple more years 'til she's legally an adult. If she wants to act like a fool then, well, there's not much I can do about it.

I'm not crazy about pulling up to the high school with a driver. People draw conclusions and I don't want anyone in my private business at the moment. I mean, only a few weeks ago I was driving a junker held together with glue and tape, and now I show up like this?

Yeah, people have big mouths, and big mouths blabber. A lot.

But it is what it is, and besides, Evie thinks it's cool.

Because of course. She's an idiot teenager.

As the driver takes us through the Alekseev's leafy neighborhood to busier streets, I dismiss my annoyance with Evie, not wanting to waste my energy on things I can't control, and go back to Kir and his dirty, filthy words.

God, that man knows how to get my motor revving.

I might be on my way to Evie's high school right now with the mission of getting her further set up for remote learning, but damn if there isn't a thrumming between my thighs, made all the more dire by the smooth vibes of the car's backseat. If I were alone right now, I'd raise the window between the front and back seat, lie down, and reach my hand into—

"What the fuck!" Evie screams, and I scream with her.

Something hits the car so hard that even though we're wearing seat belts, Evie slides into me. We hold on to each other as the car is jostled again, and just as I think we just hit a couple potholes or something, gunfire explodes the windshield, and our driver slowly falls over in his seat.

CHAPTER TWENTY-FIVE

CHARLEIGH

My God. Has he been shot? What's going on? A hundred possibilities fire through my brain in a split second, and I protectively wrap my arms around Evie, screaming in terror.

With the driver shot, the car careens off the road onto the bumpy shoulder before it sideswipes a telephone pole. In spite of the chaos, the car is slowing, so the driver must have been able to get to the brakes.

"Miss…" he says in a weak voice. "Miss Gates…"

"What?" I cry. "What's going on? What do I do?"

"There's a pistol under my seat," he says as the car rolls to a stop. "Get it, Miss Gates. Get the pistol."

Pushing Evie to the floor, I reach under his seat from behind and feel the familiar shape of the sort of gun I am being trained on. I yank on it and it snaps from whatever's holding it in place, and I see it is indeed a Glock something or other, and that it's loaded.

My hands shake violently as I remember how to unlock the gun. "Evie, call the guys, *right now*," I scream.

The driver raises his own weapon and gets off a couple shots through the windshield.

It takes a moment for my eyes to focus, but I see Dimitri and some of his men spilling out of the car that forced us off the road. They are walking toward us. The driver fires off one more shot, but he's too messed-up to really aim, and doesn't do anything more than scare them all back behind their own vehicle.

Evie's screaming into the phone for the guys to come. We aren't that far from the house, so they should be here soon. In the meantime, it looks like it's up to me to hold Dimitri and his guys back.

"I can do this," I whisper.

I force myself to relax and blow all the air out of my lungs and aim. Since the driver's fire has ceased, the guys think we're left unprotected. This is good. I'll just wait for them to get a little bit closer…

I fire and someone drops.

Holy shit.

I just shot someone. I am pretty sure I'm going to vomit, but I take a deep breath, exhale again, and get ready to shoot.

I can puke later.

But the guy I shot, whoever he is, is down and while someone is trying to revive him, the group's return fire is now coming fast and furious. There's nothing I can do except push Evie to the floor of the car and lie on top of her.

If one of us is hit, I want it to be me.

With all I've been through, this how it ends? All the shit I survived these past weeks, including being beaten almost to death, and now I'm going to be murdered like my mother and father? The universe is taking its final shit on me, delivering its parting shot, gracing me with a nice going-away present.

Fuck you very much.

But the firing ceases. It's followed by a lot of yelling, and then I hear Vadik's voice. I don't dare raise my head to see what's going on, but a car takes off, its wheels screeching as it accelerates. In seconds, I can't hear it anymore, but I still stay down, on top of my crying sister. I'm not risking getting my head blown off.

If I can help it.

The front door of the car opens, and I unsuccessfully try to stifle a shriek.

"Charleigh, Charleigh, baby, you're okay. They left."

It's Vadik's voice, and I don't think I've ever heard anything so comforting.

"Oh my God," I say, pushing myself off the floor and pulling Evie with me. I see the panic in Vadik's face and it's like looking at an angel. My shaking is uncontrollable and then my face crumbles into full-body-wracking sobs.

Vadik pries the pistol from my hand and when Niko opens the back door of the car, I jump into his arms. Either Vadik or Kir retrieves Evie from the other side, and she's shrieking too.

"Wh... what about the driver?" I stumble.

Is he going to be another Frank, killed in the line of duty for my lame ass?

I'm not sure these sacrifices are worth it.

"He's still alive," Vadik says from the front seat. "Our men are coming to take him to the hospital. Niko will take you home."

I draw a deep breath and my fear gives way to anger, which is a good thing. I need this. It gives me power. Energy. Strength. Resolve

"I'm not going home. We are not going home. Evie and I set out to take care of her education today, and that's what we are going to do. Niko, will you take us the rest of the way to the high school?" I ask, brushing at the smudges on my light-colored clothes.

I don't care if I look dirty. Let them see me like this. Let everyone see me like this. I want the world to know it can go fuck itself. It can try as hard as it wants, but I'm not being scared into hiding. I have to live my life.

I'm pissed. Fucking pissed. Pissed at Dimitri for constantly terrorizing me and pissed at the guys for letting him. With a gun in my hand today, I almost took him out. I shot someone, although I don't know who. It doesn't matter. I got someone in their group and I hope they now know I am capable of some level of self-defense. Maybe not like the pros are, but I have some smarts and can put them to use.

I'm making it clear I'm not a victim anymore. I won't roll over for them. They can come for me, but I will fight them all the way with everything I have. Hell, I almost killed Dimitri. That feels fucking awesome.

Next time I won't miss.

Vadik puts an arm around me, leading me toward Niko's car. But I shrug him off. I don't want to be comforted. I don't want sympathy.

I want revenge.

Haven't I already suffered enough? Haven't I already sacrificed enough?

It's time for the universe to fucking do something for *me*. It's my turn. And I'm tired of waiting.

As if Vadik can read my mind, he looks around to make sure Evie's not too close, and lowers his voice as he leans nearer.

"Things have changed, Charleigh," he says in a low voice.

I tilt my head at him. "Oh really? How so, Vad?" I ask sarcastically.

Yeah, things have changed. *I* have changed.

"Instead of waiting for the *Pakhan*, my brothers and I are taking action. This war over you has got to stop, and if the *Pakhan* can't or won't do anything about it, we will. It's not a hard problem to remedy, and we've been waiting long enough."

"Wait? What? You guys are taking action?" I ask, incredulous.

He nods.

There are no words to describe the weight lifted from my chest. I breath whole, long breaths, gulping at the air like I'm starving for it, and throw my arms around his neck.

"Oh, thank you, Vadik. Thank you. This is the right thing to do. I know it," I say.

I glance over at Evie, in the backseat of Niko's car, where he's trying to engage her in conversation.

She's more interested in what Vadik and I are talking about.

"We're going to destroy the man. It's been a long time coming, and there's no reason to drag it out any longer. We're as sick of this as you are. Maybe even more so."

I can see that. After all, they've been dealing with Dimitri all their lives.

Vadik is right. Enough is enough. For the first time in weeks, I feel like maybe I'm getting the break I deserve, and that the universe is listening to me for once.

Now all I have to do is convince the guys that I be the one to take down Dimitri.

Hear that, universe? I'm *back*.

CHAPTER TWENTY-SIX

NIKO

Dimitri Yegorov stores his countless smuggled goods—whether weapons, counterfeit liquor, forged art, or stolen furs—in warehouses around town. These are businesses developed and grown by his father. Not surprisingly, Dimitri's done little or nothing to cultivate them since the man's been gone. Lucky for him, his father left good managers in place when he passed, knowing his son would have little to contribute to the empire he built.

Smart thinking, that father of his. About the only thing Dimitri has ever been good for aside from creative havoc, is siphoning money out of these businesses of his father's.

My brothers and I are about to make it much more difficult for him to do this. If they have no inventory, they have no cash flow. Without cash flow, Dimitri can't survive. It's like forcing a cockroach out of hiding.

No offense to cockroaches.

His most recent attack against Charleigh was the absolute last straw. He's lucky as hell she didn't shoot his ass—her instructor says her aim is damn good for a newbie. But it's okay that she missed him, because it gives us more time to toy with him, like a cat batting around a mouse before devouring it.

The first thing we did was pay off his men to reroute his shipments. One might think that long-term employment would secure the loyalty of the men working for him, but when we waved a few hundreds in the guys' faces, they caved so fast it was hilarious.

Fuckers.

If the people working for us ever pulled this, it would be the last thing they did before being buried six feet under.

But Dimitri has not been successful fostering loyalty among his men, rumor has it, mistreating them and using his businesses as a personal ATM.

So not only is his shit going missing, but we also have some associates who've showered a few drive-by shootings on his buildings. Not to hurt anyone—

that will come later—but to send a message that the end is near.

The *Pakhan* has gotten word of this and is not happy. In fact, his second came by the club the other day, his mangled hand still in a cast, to tell us to back off. We denied everything.

Even though everyone knows it's us. Fact is, there is no one else who would go to the lengths we are, no one who hates him as much as we do, and no one with the resources to fuck him up like we can.

And no one with the balls to defy the *Pakhan*. As his second tried to threaten, we could get in big trouble, if we already aren't. But we're past the point of caring about this shit.

A man can only take so much. We've been more than patient. Any further postponing of the inevitable will make us look weak in the region, and that's not something we're willing to risk.

Of course, we aren't sharing any of this with Charleigh. She might hear bits and pieces just by virtue of being around us, but the less she knows, the better. Although she's itching to get involved. Holding her back has been like trying to cage a hungry tiger. She keeps trying to sneak in on our plans and won't listen when we say we've got everything under control.

Charleigh's circumstances have created a

monster out of her. It's both a shame and a relief—a shame that her previous innocence has been shattered, but also a relief she's developed enough street smarts to help herself if she ends up in a bad situation.

The driver from the day Charleigh was taking Evie to school, and they were attacked? He didn't make it. But, bless him, by getting a few shots off while telling Charleigh where to find a gun, he ended up saving both her and her sister.

It's a shame when we lose a guy in the line of duty. But that's what they sign up for.

Our final parting shot is happening tonight, when we are hosting a big party here at the club so we have a solid alibi.

Not that we really need one. It just makes everything more fun.

In a far cry from when she first joined us, Charleigh's looking forward to tonight's gathering, in part because not only does she have a role to play that doesn't include waiting on members or getting her ass pinched, but also because she is tasked with being the hostess to us hosts.

I love that she's coming for multiple reasons—ranging from the fact that I just plain like to look at her, to a need for everyone in our orbit to see how well she's doing in spite of the bullshit that's been going on all around her.

The stronger she is, the stronger we are.

Even the *Pakhan* is supposed to come tonight, which is a big deal because the man does not typically socialize like some others in our region. He feels it gives the impression he is not impartial when he's out at parties and such. I call bullshit. The fact is that there are some factions he'd rather hang out with than others, and he doesn't want to show favorites. But every now and then the man needs to let his hair down and when he does, there is no place he'd rather be than here with the Alekseevs. It was like this when our father was alive, and still is.

It's funny how technology has changed the way the faction operates. Back in my father's day, if they wanted to keep an eye on, say, one of Dimitri's buildings, someone would have to camp out in the woods with binoculars for potentially hours on end, no matter what the weather.

These days?

We have drones.

That's right. Fucking drones.

I don't know much about this stuff—we hired some twenty-year-old gearhead to manage this for us—but the small surveillance drones we've used are pretty fucking amazing. And tonight, they will be putting on a show for us.

While the party is underway, my brothers and I will be checking our phones to see the status of Dimitri's warehouses.

By morning, there will be nothing left of them.

I'm not one for unnecessary destruction or going overboard. I'm the calm, rational one of my brothers, and it's usually my job to rein them in. But about this maneuver, I am almost giddy, like a kid on Christmas eve, waiting for Santa to come.

This is way better than Santa, though.

While we haven't gotten to the final blow we will be dealing Dimitri, the one where he meets his maker, this second to last is the most… explosive.

Yes, we are fucking blowing up all his buildings. And it will be caught on film, memorialized like some kind of Oscar-winning picture.

We're about an hour out from our strike when Charleigh arrives, and fuck if she doesn't stun.

How is it this woman gets more beautiful every time I see her? How is it even possible?

Tonight, her hair is styled into a sleek, high ponytail that leaves her long, milky neck exposed. Her shimmery dress leaves nearly all her back exposed, showing off her flawless skin. It drapes over her ass as she walks and is just snug enough that I can see the tiny jiggle of her flesh as she moves.

But it's the front of the dress that almost knocks me to my knees. While it ties behind her neck, its V center is cut down almost to her navel. The thin fabric barely restrains her small breasts, which are firm and pointed, like always.

"Hey," she says, nudging me. "Cat got your tongue?" she asks like a wise ass.

I tear my eyes away to greet a guest. The moment he's gone, I am back to her. "Fuck all, baby. What do you say to someone who looks like you? I can't even think of a compliment that will do you justice. So I won't even bother trying. I'll just stare at you all night long."

She drops her head back and laughs softly, exposing that neck I am dying to run my lips over. But there will be time for that later, and I need to stop thinking with my little head.

"There's a guard over there," I say, discreetly gesturing with my chin. "He will be keeping an eye on you all night, even if you're just going to the ladies' room. So, please mingle. My brothers and I have a little business to attend to."

Her eyes widen. "Really? What? What are you doing so late at night?"

Her face is so eager I hate to shut her down, but

there's no way she needs to know about the operation before it takes place.

"You'll find out later," I say, kissing her temple and running my palm over her soft ass.

"Well," she shrugs. "Off I go." And she crosses the room toward some of the men she used to serve drinks to. On her way, every head turns to admire her.

She doesn't even notice.

I glad hand a few more guests when Kir texts me. I make sure no one sees me and meet him in Vadik's office, where we pull up the surveillance from our drones. And sure enough, Dimitri's buildings are being leveled one by one, in sequence, like a row of dominoes that falls over until nothing is left standing.

When the last one falls, my brothers and I are quiet.

We could jump up and down, high five each other, and generally act like jackasses. But we don't. This is our job. This is what we do. We succeeded in this mission because we always succeed.

And we will succeed in ending Dimitri's life.

The *Pakhan* made his appearance and left, having been charmed by the lovely Charleigh, their conflict of the week before if not forgotten, then swept under the rug for the evening. He was jovial and even allowed our girl to fawn over him a bit, not that any man could resist her. But she's learning, and she knows he's important in our world, even if they don't always see eye to eye.

It's one a.m., and while some of our guests have hit the road, the real night owls are still arriving, like a shift change or something. I'm not sure how much longer I'll last, to be honest, because I was up very early with work involving the attack on Dimitri's properties. Now that they are demolished, we are in a delicate phase for a few days where, until we get him, we're vulnerable to all sorts of attacks. But that's okay. Our security is beefed up nicely and I'm confident all will be fine.

Until it's not.

Just a few minutes past two a.m., there is a rat-a-tat-tat out in front of our building. While the noise is not loud, almost like a small firecracker, my instincts fire on all cylinders and I run to check our security camera footage.

Fuck all.

I race downstairs with my brothers in time to see a car full of bullet holes roll to a complete stop and come to rest against a stop sign. A quick inventory of the situation shows that in front of the club, we have some members down, and that our ace security team has riddled the attacker's car with bullets, taking out all its occupants.

Mother fuckers.

Charleigh dashes outside and screams when she sees the bodies and puddles of blood on our front steps.

"*You*," I holler at one of the security guys, "take Miss Gates to the compound *now*. Make sure she gets to her room. Charleigh, call me when you're there and check on your sister."

Charleigh hesitates for a moment, then runs as best she can in her heels to catch up with the bodyguard, who loads her into the back seat of one of our SUVs and screeches out of the lot.

I look at my brothers.

"The fucker," Kir says. "It's almost like he was ready for us."

We look at each other in silence for a moment, and then Vadik speaks.

"Maybe he was ready for us. And if that's the case, who helped him get ready?

CHAPTER TWENTY-SEVEN

Niko

The dead guys in the sniper car had no ID or fingerprints, probably cheap hires whose expendable lives no one gives a shit about. The three of them are now loaded with lead, doubled over in the late-model BMW they were driving, which turns out to be stolen.

I call the *Pakhan*. "I'm sorry to wake you, sir. It's Niko Alekseev. There was a hit on the club tonight. I thought you should know, especially since you were here earlier."

This gets his attention.

Was someone trying to take him out? Or is this just a random message from a rival wanting to show he can fuck us up just as much as we can him?

Either way, no one gets away with this.

"Any casualties?" the *Pakhan* asks.

"Yes, sir. Three club members were hit on their way in. Our security guards got the shooters' car. All of them are deceased."

He's silent, then takes a deep breath. "Okay. Get rid of all the bodies. I will ask around, and you do the same. Let me know what you find out."

"Will do, sir."

I return to my brothers who are overseeing the cleanup. "Anyone in the club know this is going on?"

Vadik shakes his head. "I don't think so. Which means we need to get this cleaned up and get back in there and act like everything is fine. What did the *Pakhan* say?" he asks.

I shrug. "Not much. You know he's not a man of many words. But I have a feeling we'll be hearing more from him. This hit a little too close for comfort, given that he was actually here tonight."

"Any ID on the car?" Kir asks.

I run my fingers through my hair. The truth is, I really just want to go home and get to bed. But duty calls. "Not a thing. Dimitri was smart enough to remove every last bit of identifying information, even from the men. There's not a complete fingertip among the three of them."

I don't know what Dimitri is thinking. I really don't. Each one of these hits puts him closer and closer to his grave. He can't possibly think we won't know it's him. And yet he keeps striking, even when we've destroyed both his supply chain and his inventory and warehouses. The man is essentially out of business now.

That could be why he's fighting like he has nothing to lose. There's really not much left for the man. Which means he will only get more and more reckless. More and more dangerous.

It's never been more imperative that we find him once and for all. Get this shit over and done so we can move on with our lives.

Next day, I get a frantic call from Evie. She's never called me before.

"What going on, honey? Everything all right?" I ask.

She's hyperventilating. "I... I was up front at the guard's shack just talking, and I saw something. I saw something awful, Niko."

Leave it to the kid to make friends with the security team. I make a mental note to talk to them about not falling for her teenage charms. She may be cute, but she's not someone they ought to get close to.

"Evie, are you back in the house now?" I ask.

First things first.

"Yeah. The guards brought me back. I think they are out front checking it out. But I wanted to call you."

"Okay. Okay, good. Where is your sister, Evie?"

"Um, she's in the shower. I haven't told her yet."

"Okay. Now tell me what you saw," I say.

Her breath is still coming hard. I hope like hell she says she saw a dead squirrel or something.

"Well, I… think it was a hand. It was kind of hard to tell. It was so messed up and bloody."

Shit. Shit, shit, shit.

I have a feeling I know what she saw.

"Okay, look Evie. I'll call the security guards. But do me a favor and stay in the house until we get home, okay?" I ask.

"Y… yeah. Okay, Niko."

"All right, sweetie. Bye."

I find my brothers. "Guys. We have a situation. Another goddamn situation."

I fill my brothers in.

"Do you think it's our guy? The one we sent after Arseny, in the hospital?"

I nod. "I'm pretty sure. What we know is that the operation was bungled. Not only did they not get through to Arseny, but they gave chase and I guess the guy whose body parts are in front of our house is the one who didn't manage to get away."

Vadik drops his face into his hands. "Good God. We go to take out the asshole Charleigh shot in the hold up and we couldn't even get close to the punk? Guys, are our people falling down on the job or what?"

I hate to admit it, I mean really, really hate to goddamn admit it, but Dimitri may be turning out to be a bigger foe than we ever gave him credit for. I'm surprised. But I've also always loved a challenge.

"Does Charleigh know yet?" Kir asks.

"Evie told me she's in the shower. But I'm sure she'll tell her when she gets out."

Shit. We didn't want Charleigh to know about this latest strike. Not that she has any say, but she's not going to like our going after Arseny. She doesn't understand our world, and certainly doesn't understand why we'd go after someone she's already shot when Dimitri is the person we want.

I look at my phone, which I know will ring momentarily. She's going to have questions. I'll be honest with her. I always am. She's not going to like what she hears.

As long as she's part of our world, she's going to witness—both see and hear—a lot of things she doesn't like.

CHAPTER TWENTY-EIGHT

Charleigh

"Arseny? Why go after Arseny?" I ask.

What the hell? He's a low-level punk. Why waste the manpower? And now one man is dead, chopped up and left as bait at the front gate of the compound.

Whose remains, by the way, were found by my *sister.*

Such. Bullshit.

As if the kid is not already traumatized enough, she gets to see a mangled, bloody hand, separated from its body.

I swear to God, I am ready to take all the cash I can muster, put Evie in a car, and drive straight to Mexico, where we'll hide for the rest of our lives.

Living like this is not sustainable. It's deadly. If

one of the Alekseev's rivals doesn't get us, the stress from the fear will.

Then I think about what it would be like to never feel Vadik's, Kir's, or Niko's arms around me again, and I hate myself for being weak. A few months ago, I didn't even know these men existed. Now I don't think I can live without them.

Last night, when I got home after the horrible drive by that took several club members' lives, first thing I did was check on Evie. Of course. There was a guard sitting outside her door, I was happy to see, and after peeking in on her, I thanked the man and went to my own room.

But there was no sleeping. After tossing and turning for a bit, I got up and paced my room. I even considered walking the grounds, but I wasn't feeling safe enough for that. So, I bolted over to the cottage where Niko stays, and climbed into his bed to wait for him to get home.

Through his big glass doors, there were bits and pieces of the evening's moon flashing through the tree canopy. Something about that, along with being in Niko's bed, soothed me. I finally dozed off and barely stirred when he came to bed at four am—or was it five?

He must have showered before he joined me, because he was still wet and smelled so good, just clean, simple soap, and even though his skin was chilled, I rolled right into his arms and went back to sleep.

Simply put, it was heavenly, especially after such a fucked-up night.

I don't know how much time passed, but when I was gently woken, the room was full of light and Niko was next to me, his face covered in concern.

"Baby, wake up," he said. "You're having a nightmare."

It took a moment to shift from seeing Dimitri stare down at me with his evil eyes, to realizing I was safe and in the arms of Niko.

"Oh, thank God," I said, snuggling into him. "Thank you for waking me."

He flipped me over on my side and we spooned for a while, until I felt his growing erection bumping against my behind. I turned to face him and with only a smile let him know what I wanted.

Without breaking our gaze, he rolled on top of me and, balancing on one arm, pushed my nightie to my waist. I wrapped my legs around him and placed my hands on either side of his face, tracing his heavy brow with my thumbs.

I'm learning that sometimes sex is hard, fast, dirty, and loud—and sometimes it's not. This was one of those times.

I push Niko's blond hair off his handsome forehead and laugh when it falls right back down. I want to kiss every inch of his face, he's so perfect, and the love he has in his eyes is so deep it almost hurts my heart.

Because I know I feel the same way. Not that I'm telling him. Yet. I'm simply not ready.

His hard cock finds my wet entrance and slides inside in one smooth movement. I close my eyes and drop my head back onto the pillow beneath me, ready to sail away to that place where life is perfect and any worries or sadnesses are so far out of sight it's like they don't even exist.

Niko strokes my inner walls, pulling all the way out and then driving back inside with a steady rhythm. I open my eyes for a moment to find him watching me, measuring my response, like it's not enough to be inside my pussy, but he also wants to be inside my head to know my thoughts and feel my feelings.

I never expected this level of intimacy from any of the Alekseev brothers, and yet here we are. I close my eyes again, because I'm not quite ready to engage at this level. I may never be. But for now, Niko's gentle fucking is all I need, the perfect antidote to waking up from a terrifying nightmare and a delicious way to start the day.

Does it disappoint him that I don't return his desire for connection? It's hard to tell. He's an intuitive man, sensitive, at least as compared to his brothers. He sees things they don't, and that's part of the reason he's such a good addition to the trio.

I wonder if his rocky beginnings, trying to find a place in a family where he's an accidental afterthought, afforded him these skills, the kind that help an outsider fit in. In some regards I see myself the same. Growing up, I was always the kid people felt sorry for because I had no mother, and was a weirdo because my father owned a pawn shop.

That must be why, when I started my bookkeeping classes and found I had an affinity for the subject, I dove in, hook, line, and sinker. I was going to change how the world saw me, and especially how I saw myself.

All that's off the table now, but I hope with the help of the guys, I can find my footing again.

My orgasm begins with a tingling, like an electric current that makes your hair stand on end, and I grip Niko's ass to pull him deeper inside me. He gets the message and starts to pound me, shaking the bed and the wall it's slamming against.

We don't care.

"Oh God, Niko," I murmur, "I'm coming, yes, fuck me."

Niko erupts into an explosive groan and with a few more strokes holds himself deep inside me while we come at the same time. It's transcendent, and I'm grateful for the few moments away from reality to the beautiful place only he can take me.

CHAPTER TWENTY-NINE

Charleigh

I'm still not happy about the Alekseev's attempt on Arseny's life. The fact that they didn't succeed means we have to be on higher alert than ever, as if that's possible. Their excuse is that no one is innocent in their world, and that everyone knows the risks.

War is messy, I've heard Vadik say more than once.

I let Evie talk me into allowing her to attend some school play that her friends are in. It's only a couple hours long, and the guys had the security team sweep the place before it got started, and assigned them with staying there until it's time to come home. I'm not completely comfortable with this outing. Evie knows that, the security team knows that, and the guys know that. And yet they all pretty much overruled my objections, even after all the attempts on our lives.

Knowing Dimitri's businesses are pretty much destroyed due to the Alekseev's bombing of his warehouses has left me sitting on pins and needles. If we don't take the man out soon, he'll have another chance to strike.

I am not made for this strange world I've fallen into.

One of the conditions under which I agreed to let Evie attend her school thing was if I could attend also. Of course, she had a dozen reasons why I shouldn't but they really boiled down to the fact that it wouldn't 'look cool' to her friends for her big sister to be there, and that she doesn't 'need a babysitter.'

Tough shit.

After all we've been through, I'd think the kid might have developed some common sense.

But no.

I stand in the back of the auditorium with an assortment of teachers and parents, and nod at the educators who were on staff when I was in high school. They are all too aware that Evie is very different from me, and that's why I'm so hands-on with her.

The lights in the auditorium go dark, and the stage lights up. Before they did, I had a pretty clear view of Evie, but now without light, I can't really keep an eye on her.

I'm hoping someone from the security team can.

It's a cute performance these high schoolers are putting on, and as I relax, I'm glad Evie insisted on attending. She needs to get out of the house and be around people her age. Homeschooling is not a long-term solution, not for a girl like her who needs to socialize and spread her wings.

And just as I'm getting into the play, which is really well done, there is a scream from the front of the audience.

It could be nothing, but high alert is my new normal. I stand on my tiptoes and crane my neck and then there is more screaming, followed by the scraping of chairs, and the players onstage stop what they're doing to watch something going on in the front rows.

The heavy auditorium doors burst open and the Alekseev security team flies in, weapons drawn.

No. Please, no. Not here.

This is my sister's sanctuary. The only place where she feels like a normal teenager. It's bad enough so much has been taken from me, but really?

A sixteen-year-old girl? Where is the fairness in that? And when does it stop?

"Get the lights!" I shout and push my way to the front of the auditorium.

But when security sees me, they surround me and start to usher me out of the room.

I fight back. "Where is my sister? We have to get my sister first!" I scream.

"We've got her, Miss Gates, she's right over here," someone says, and Evie runs at me so hard she almost knocks me over.

With my arms around her, I survey the pandemonium in the room. Kids are trying to get out, but the ancient folding chairs they were in are falling over, causing everybody to trip. The teachers in the back are trying to get some sort of control of the room but their instructions are drowned out by all the noise. It's when I hear gunshots outside, coming from the parking lot, that I understand why the security team has barred the doors, pushing back on the panicked teenagers.

This is awful. Ugly. And it's all our fault.

These kids do not deserve this. Neither do the teachers, or parents, or anybody else. They are innocent.

Am I going to go through life afraid to go out

because of the trouble I might bring to others? Is that a way to live?

I look up at the guard who's pulled Evie and me into a corner of the room, blocking anyone from seeing us with his huge body. "What's going on? How will we get out of here?" I cry.

He brings his watch to his mouth and I realize he's wearing a wire. He's communicating with someone, somewhere. "It will be over soon, Miss Gates. But it looks like someone was coming for your sister."

I don't understand how anyone outside our tight group of the Alekseevs, us, and security could even know where Evie was going tonight.

And now there's a shootout in front of the high school. It's like I not only have a black cloud hanging over my head, but I am also spreading it wherever I go.

CHAPTER THIRTY

Charleigh

"Can I sleep with you in your bed tonight, Char?" Evie asks, a long way from the smart-ass teenager she was earlier in the evening.

I look at her standing in my bedroom doorway, her face scrubbed clean of the black shit she rings her eyes with, in her striped pajamas, carrying the teddy bear she got from our mother. I push the comforter back on the empty side of my bed and wave her in.

"Thanks, Char," she says, smiling as she scoots under the covers with me.

I snuggle up next to her and stroke her hair, hoping it will help her sleep. As for me, I think I'll probably lie awake all night.

All of a sudden, my bedroom door flies open. "Charleigh, have you seen—" Kir starts to say.

Evie and I both raise our heads and he backs out of the room with a wave. "Oh, there you are. Goodnight, ladies," he says, pulling the door closed.

"Hey, Char," Evie says.

"Yeah?"

"Those guys like you. Like, really like you."

Damn. Guess it's pretty obvious.

"You think?" I ask, hoping to end the conversation before it gets started.

"Oh my God, Char. Duh!"

Evie drops off to sleep while I recount the aftermath of tonight's attack. After she and I were rushed home, Vadik came by to fill me in. Turned out one of the guys after Evie was shot dead and the other got away. The man who was killed had no identification or fingerprints, which seems par for the course in this world.

So bizarre. I mean, I don't even want to think about how one removes their fingerprints.

Vadik told me Evie and I can't leave the house for a while because things between the rival factions are escalating at such a rapid pace. No surprise there. I just wish the guys would let me be part of the war. Vadik nearly burst out laughing when I suggested that, but quickly reassured me as soon as I'm ready, I will be welcome to join the team.

I'll believe that when I see it.

Next morning, after an entire night of insomnia and stewing over things, I confront the guys when they come to the kitchen for morning coffee. I don't care who hears what I have to say.

Hands on hips, I march up to the three of them. "Are you guys putting off the inevitable again? Are you not going after Dimitri because of something the *Pakhan* is telling you? Are you keeping something from me?"

The guys look at each other with raised eyebrows. "Well. Good morning to you too," Kir says, topping off his coffee. "Damn," he mumbles under his breath.

"I heard that."

A titter passes through the kitchen staff but when I turn to see what's going on, not a single soul has lifted their head from their work.

Whatever.

"Hey, Char. Give the guys a break."

I turn to see Evie, scarfing down her breakfast bagel and juice, pointing a finger at me like a scolding school teacher.

Seriously?

"Char," she continues, "it's partly my fault for insisting on going to the play. I should have just listened to you and sucked it up and stayed home. Look, you need to find a balance between happiness and revenge."

Well, that just about shuts everybody up. The brothers look amused and excuse themselves to get to work, and I stand there in the kitchen having been admonished by about the most immature, impractical teenager in the world.

"Wait here," I say to Evie, and run after the guys, who are getting in their cars.

"Hey," I call after them. "Don't think what my sister just said gets you off the hook. I'm not leaving you alone until this matter is resolved one way or the other. If not just for my sake and my sister's, but what about Stacey? What about Clara?" I ask, looking directly at Kir.

A dark cloud passes over his face, and I realize I probably went too far. But I have to let the guys know I'm fucking serious, and this business of waiting is getting very old.

"I want to know what's going on!" I scream.

Vadik approaches me with his hands up like he's surrendering. "Charleigh, Charleigh, please calm down."

Oh my God. Did he really just say that? Does he not know that the worst thing to tell a not-calm person is to calm down? That's like throwing gasoline on a freaking fire.

I know he's smarter than that.

"Why, Vadik? Why should I calm down? Personally, I can't think of a single reason why I shouldn't be upset and yelling at the top of my lungs."

He's not pleased and his reconciliation posture changes as he approaches me, finger pointing at my face. "Look. You *will* follow our lead. You *will* follow our instructions. And you *will* not speak to any of us that way unless you want to be indefinitely locked in your room."

Holy hell. Would they really do that?

Best not to test them.

"I… I can't let this go," I say, forcing calm into my voice. "I know my sister has a point, but I can't be happy without revenge. It's choking me. It's taken over every aspect of my life. I think about it all day and dream about it all night. You probably think I'm obsessed. Well, you would be right. I am."

I look from one of them to the next, and the care in their eyes moves me to tears. That's when I realize, finally realize, that they *are* listening to me, that they have been listening to me all along, and that maybe the person who hasn't been paying attention is me.

Maybe it's time for me to shut my mouth and really hear what they are saying, that they love me, would do anything for me, and that they have my back.

CHAPTER THIRTY-ONE

Charleigh

Low and behold, when I finally do start listening, what I find out is exactly what I was hoping to hear all along.

"When was the last time he was seen?" Niko asks.

There is a pause. I want to peek around the corner from where I'm eavesdropping just outside the library, but I figure if the guys wanted me in on this conversation, they would have included me.

I was headed to the kitchen for some tea, having tossed and turned all night in bed—again. It's so early the sun's not up yet, but I'm hoping something minty might help me relax and get a couple hours' sleep before I start the day.

It's strange the guys are up so early.

"According to our men, he hasn't been here in a long time. Like weeks, maybe even months. He's hiding out somewhere," Kir says, "which is smart because he knows he'd be a dead man, otherwise."

"Yeah, he has people helping him for sure. He couldn't do this on his own. He'd need support," Niko adds.

I want to walk in on the guys. I want to join the conversation, be part of this, whatever it is they are talking about and planning. I need the peace of mind that will come with knowing I've done what I can to make myself and my sister safe, or as safe in this world as we can be.

And yet, the guys keep cutting me out. They'll say it's for my own good—I'm not ready yet, I don't understand their world, blah, blah, blah. They may be right. But I don't really care. I know what I need and no one is going to get it for me, except me. I've always been alone in this world. Why should things be any different now?

But in case the guys are still inclined to cut me out, which it seems they are, I continue listening.

"So why bother going over, if we know he's not there?" Vadik asks.

"We've discussed this," Kir says. "Charleigh remembers some sort of private room from when she was there. We need to see if it holds anything that might link him to our parents' murders. We take that to the *Pakhan*, and all this bullshit will be over."

Or, they tip Dimitri off and he leaves the country never to be heard from again. Which wouldn't be such a bad thing, excepts he has tentacles that reach anywhere he wants, just like the Alekseev brothers do.

God, I'm starting to think like they do. I don't like it. In fact, it makes me feel sick.

"Fine then," Vadik says. "Let's head over there in twenty. If the guys watching the house say it's okay."

"They've been watching it. Seems no one's around."

I race back up to my room before I'm discovered, but I'm not fast enough.

"Charleigh, hey. What are you doing up so early?" Kir calls after me.

I look back down the stairs as I continue to my room. "Oh hey. Morning. I can't sleep, so thought I'd get some tea."

He tilts his head. "Where's the tea?"

Shit.

"Oh, we don't have what I wanted, so I bailed on the idea. See ya later," I say, closing my bedroom door.

I pull on some jeans and a sweatshirt and my trusty old Converse Chucks, and peek back out my door. The guys have all dispersed to do whatever they have to before heading over Dimitri's. I grab a book in case I come across someone, so I can say I'm going to read for a bit, and sneak down the stairs and out the front door. Just as I hoped, one of their SUVs is parked in the drive with engine already running. I take a look around and with no one in the vicinity, open the back and scramble in, plastering myself against the backside of the rear seat.

I'm not fooling anyone, though. All they have to do is glance in the trunk area and I'll be discovered.

Still, when I hear their voices drawing near, I make myself as small as possible. I squeeze my eyes closed—why, I have no idea—and force my breath to slow, as if that will possibly help.

And to my surprise, the guys hop in without noticing me. I brace myself so I don't roll when they peel out, and we hit the road.

Holy shit. What have I done? To be honest, I didn't really think this was going to work. And now here I am.

What will the guys do when they find out I'm a stowaway? Will they be pissed or just mildly annoyed? Will they take to locking me in my room like they did in the beginning, or will they be pleased with my initiative?

Kind of late to worry about it now. I'm freaking committed.

With my head plastered to the floor of the trunk, I try not to think about how many dead bodies have been back here. The carpet smells vaguely of chemicals, so I guess if there was anything incriminating around, it's been cleaned to within an inch of its life.

But still. Gross.

The guys' voices carry over the rumble of the engine, but the noise drowns out anything specific. The mention of my name pricks my ears a few times, but I hear nothing more than that.

After thirty minutes or so—I tracked the time as well as our location with my phone—the SUV comes to a stop.

Oh shit. Now what?

I'm such a fucking idiot.

Sure, I'll go for a ride to the home of the man who's been after me since the first time we met, who beat me to within an inch of my life, and whose people also recently tried to nab my sister, Evie. The man who is responsible for the murder of the Alekseev brothers' parents, for whom the *Pakhan*—for some incomprehensible reason—is protecting or at least keeping our thirst for revenge against at bay.

Yeah. Let's go over to his house. Take a look around. See what we find.

What could possibly go wrong?

The SUV doors open and I know I need to reveal myself. Waiting could make things much worse. What if they take me for an intruder, or I need protecting and they don't even know I'm nearby?

"Guys," I hiss.

Vadik and Niko have already exited the front seat, so only Kir hears me. He whips around at the same time he draws his weapon.

"WHAT THE FUCK, CHARLEIGH?" he hollers when he sees me peeking over the seat.

Don't make yourself small. Ask for what you want. You deserve it. And you can have it. I raise my chin. "You're not doing this without me."

The truck opens and Vadik and Kir are standing there. They don't look happy. "I… I thought you were in bed," Kir says.

"I *was*. And now I'm not," I say, scrambling out of the back. "I need a gun."

The three of them look like I'm crazy.

They are not far off.

Vadik shakes his head slowly. "No. Absolutely not. I'm calling one of the security guys to come get you right now. Niko, wait with her."

I get right up in Vadik's face. "That's bullshit. I'm ready for this and you know it."

He inhales slowly and deeply, like the parent of a toddler trying to keep their shit together. Which makes me all the more pissed. "I'm sorry, Charleigh. I know you want this. Hell, you're risking your life right now by being here with us.

I poke him in the chest with my forefinger. I don't know who I surprised more, him or myself. "There. You just said it. If I'm risking my life, you know you are too."

He grabs my hand off his chest and whips it up behind my back. I can't move and while it doesn't hurt, it's not comfortable, either.

Fine. He's got me.

He gets right in my face. "You will wait here with Niko. You are highly vulnerable right now and need to get the hell out of here. And I don't want to hear anything more about it. Understand?" he growls, so close that his breath is warm on my face.

"Yes," I whisper, defeated.

"Now get back in the SUV," he says.

I crawl into the backseat, fighting back tears, and Niko slides in next to me. With my arms crossed tightly, I look out the window, wishing I could disappear into a hole in the ground.

Yes, I am fucking humiliated. These guys treat me

like a child. They don't take me seriously. And I'm sick of it.

Niko's fingertips brush my thigh, and I scoot further away from him. The last thing I want right now is any attempt by anyone to comfort me.

He sighs and pulls his hand back. "Charleigh. I know what it's like to feel left out."

"No, you don't," I snap.

"Hey. You don't know what it's like to be me, to be the bastard son of a family like this. You never fully feel like you belong, no matter how long and hard you work to prove yourself. I've inherited an empire that I'll never really feel belongs to me, like I'm some sort of hanger-on. Sometimes, like when I stay busy, I don't think about it, at least not for a long time. But it's always there, the nagging doubts, like do I deserve this, have I earned it, and do I really belong here. My brothers and parents have never treated me like I'm anything less than a full member of the family, and yet, my illegitimacy hangs over my head like an annoying cloud," he says.

I finally look at him. I get the point he's making, and yet our situations are so different, I don't see how he can compare them.

Five minutes later, one of the compound's security guys shows up. I mutter a *see you later* over my shoulder to Niko, because I can't bear to give him anything more.

He might like some reassurance that I understand, that the rules have sunk in, and that I have accepted my proper place in this small family, but I can't give him that.

After all, if I don't believe it myself, how can I convince him of it?

CHAPTER THIRTY-TWO

Vadik

Dimitri's house—or should I say his father's house—is much the same as it was when we came over as kids, when our fathers used to do business together and our families gathered for holidays and such.

Strange, to think that the man I'm ready to sacrifice anything for to get him off this earth was once a childhood friend.

Not that my brothers and I liked him much when we were kids. He was a spoiled, pain in the ass, whiny boy, and we teased him mercilessly. Maybe it's no wonder we grew up to hate each other.

But the hate, the hard-core part of it, anyway, didn't really start until his father died and left his share of the club to Papa, completely overlooking and passing over Dimitri. The humiliation he experienced when that happened turned someone already prone to bitterness and animosity into a monster of epic proportions. He went from being merely annoying to unbearable, unwilling or unable to accept that his father didn't leave him the club because he was sure he'd only run it into the ground.

The truth hurts, sometimes so much that we tell ourselves lies about it.

So Dimitri chose to believe our father stole the club out from under him, rather than what was clearly written in his father's will in plain black and white—that Dimitri was bequeathed all the other less consequential family businesses, just not the club that our fathers founded together. The fact that everyone in our world knew what happened and why, heightened Dimitri's humiliation, and his anger eventually pushed him over the edge. When it comes down to it, the man really just flat out lost his shit. It's not uncommon for men in our world to become unhinged, but the natural order of things, because these men are so volatile and unpredictable, dictates that their days are numbered. They are just too much of a risk to keep around.

We let him come around the club though, in the spirit of temporarily keeping the peace. Turned out that even that charitable gesture bit us in the ass, something that seldom happens because we see most shit coming our way well before it reaches us.

Bottom line is, the man is no end of trouble, has been for a long time, and the end that is coming his way is inevitable and well-deserved. It aways has been, even going back to before his father died.

Maybe his father knew and that's why he didn't leave him the club.

But none of that is my problem, at least it won't be for much longer. Today, Kir and I—while Niko waits for Charleigh the stowaway to get a ride back to the compound—are inside Dimitri's house looking for some hidden room to see if it might get us closer to the bastard, or at least closer to proving he murdered our parents.

What might it hold that no other room does? I have no freaking idea, except for the hunch that I'm going on.

Papa taught me to listen to my hunches. They may not always be accurate, he said, but they are there for a reason.

Problem is, my hunch is also telling me we might have made a mistake coming here today, even though our advance team assured us the coast was clear.

Kir and I are quiet. Actually, more than quiet. Years of practice allows us to enter just about any place undetected. But, guns drawn, we move through the familiar house, and in the reflection of a window, I see the butt of another gun waiting for my brother and me to round the corner. I stop in my tracks and with a minuscule shake of my head, Kir understands we're not alone.

From where we stand, I watch the gun move, as well as the man holding it, probably some hired lackey who doesn't get paid enough for the shitty risks he has to take to put food on the table. But that's not my problem right now.

Staying alive is.

While we have this guy in our sights, the advantage is ours because he is unaware that we do. The question is, are there others?

There most likely are.

A place like this would never be guarded by only one guy.

I'm not pleased our advance team didn't pick up on the fact that there were men waiting here for us, ready to ambush. But again, that is something I will have to deal with later.

I could take out the man approaching us right now, and that would be the end of him, but that would also give away our position to anyone else in the house. I'm not usually one to hesitate—neither is my brother Kir—but we need to weigh the risks we're facing.

I mouth *Niko* to Kir, and he nods, holstering his gun and grabbing his phone to send a text. He's done in under fifteen seconds, weapon back in hand, and I feel much better that Niko knows what we are facing inside.

I just don't know if Charleigh has gone back to the compound yet. If not, I'm not so sure I want him to leave her alone.

But the options swirling in my head force action when the gunman we're watching begins to round the corner. Before he can even register my brother and me waiting for him, a gun fires. The man's eyes widen in surprise as his body arcs forward. He stumbles, then falls to his knees, and I kick the gun out of his hand beyond his reach.

Kir covers me while I do this, and when the man falls, I can see behind him, explaining where the shot came from.

Behind him, at the end of the hallway, is Charleigh, pistol drawn, standing in perfect shooting posture.

Holy shit.

She has a lot of explaining to do.

CHAPTER THIRTY-THREE

VADIK

Niko steps from behind her.

I'm going to kill him. He may be my brother but I'm going to kill him, letting Charleigh take the first shot when Kir and I were pretty much sitting ducks?

"C'mon. We've gotta get out of here," he says. "There are others on the way."

We look outside and when the coast looks clear, sprint to the SUV and take off. Barely a word is uttered until we return to the compound, aside from Niko taking Charleigh's gun away from her.

We pull into the drive in front of the house and I jam the car into park. I am out of my mind furious and before we even reach the front door, I explode.

"I'd like to know what the fuck happened back there," I say, glaring at Niko and Charleigh.

My fists are balled so tightly it's like my fingers are breaking. Despite the pain, I can't force them to relax.

Kir puts a hand on my back. "Hey, let's all go inside. We'll talk in the library."

Without a word, I storm into the house, the others following. I head straight to the bar cart, pour myself a scotch even though it's still early morning, and realize as soon as I get a whiff of it, it's the last thing I want right now. My stomach flips, and I can taste bile in my throat, and then, without even thinking about it, I heave the glass against the wood paneled wall, sending booze and slivers of glass all over.

Niko and Kir stand there, staring at me like they are daring me to do it again. They're pissed at my tantrum.

Charleigh, however, vacillates between bravery and terror.

I pace the room a few times, trying to get my shit together. It's not working.

"What the fuck was that?" I holler.

Niko raises his hands as if that's going to help me calm down, then drops them and shakes his head.

Yeah, I'm hopeless when I'm like this. I know it. We all know it. I have to work through it.

"Now, Vad, you might think letting Charleigh

take that guy down was some sort of rash decision, but it wasn't. Look, you don't know this, but I've been training her myself. I knew she could do it, so that's why I let her. When the security guy came to take her away, I decided she didn't need to go."

Charleigh looks up from the club chair she settled into, her chin high. "Vadik, I'm ready, and I just proved that to you. If Niko hadn't given me the chance, I never would have been able to show you."

"Bullshit," I yell. "It might have been a calculated risk, but there was no reason to take one to begin with. Kir and I could have been killed."

"But you weren't. You weren't because I was there, acting as part of the team. I knew I could take that guy out and any other guys there. It's what I've been training for, Vadik."

Her soft voice helps my anger ebb, but only a little. Am I angry because I'm afraid Charleigh won't need me anymore? That she's taking away my ability to die defending her because she can fend for herself now?

Am I more worried about the danger all this poses to Charleigh herself than any of the three of us?

Goddamn, this is all so fucked.

I take a seat in the corner and drop my head into my hands. Fuck, I am so not in the mood for one of my migraines. I fish into my pocket for a pill and swallow it without water.

Tastes like shit.

I look up to see Charleigh standing over me and when she places a hand on my shoulder, my own immediately goes to hers as if she might transfer some peace to me.

Her fingers are small but warm, and I bring her hand to my lips for a kiss. Her skin is soft and smells fresh, lightly scented as if from simple drugstore hand lotion. It's one of the things I like best about her. She doesn't try too hard to be attractive, in fact, she barely makes any effort at all, which makes her all the more appealing. She's so incredibly different from the usual tarted-up women I cross paths with.

Keeping this woman alive has not been an easy feat. Our rivals have found a chink in our armor, our affection for this woman, and they are exploiting it every way they can. If she's to remain a part of our lives, which I hope to God she is, she needs to be able to defend herself.

And today she proved she can.

Then why am I so tweaked about it? I want her safe, and I want her to be able to keep herself safe.

Guess that means she might not need me quite as much as she has, and that has me feeling a little bitch-ass apprehensive.

Which I don't like. Not at all.

I don't get worked up over women, even the ones I'm fucking.

At least I never have.

Charleigh stands before me in her jeans and sneakers looking for all the world like a queen, my queen, a Bratva queen, and an Alekseev queen. She stills my rage while stoking my fire, if that makes sense at all, and as soon as I put my hands on her hips to pull her to me, rubbing my rough thumbs over her hipbones, my cock jumps to attention.

I've let Charleigh have some space these recent weeks, just like my brothers have. We've followed her lead, let her come to us for her sensual needs, always ready to help her heal in any way we can.

And today she's doing the same for me.

I open her jeans, and pulling them just below her ass, reach into the tight space between her legs. I run a finger through her bare pussy lips, and it comes back coated with her excitement. I taste her and it's good, so good I know I want more, I need more, I have to have more.

My brothers settle into chairs to watch as I lay Charleigh back on the thick rug below us. Flipping her over, I keep her jeans around her thighs, binding her legs tightly together. Her movement is restricted and yet she still wags her behind, offering herself to me, while I pull my trousers off and toss them aside. Straddling her ass, I push into the snug space where her thighs meet, and slide in and out of that void, teasing us both to the point where we can't take it any longer.

With her legs pressed together, I enter her and am immediately enveloped with her slick, heavenly heat, her pussy grabbing for my cock like a hungry little bird begging for all I have to give.

Beneath me, Charleigh slaps and bangs her hands on the rug under her, arching her neck, and throwing her hair around in response to my drilling. She manages to push one hand beneath herself to play with her clit, and I drive in and out of her faster, matching her groans, when she clamps down on me and comes, her cheek pressed to the rug, her lips parted, and her eyes only partially open.

"Yes, Vad, please fuck me," she pleads as another orgasm rolls over her.

I let her finish and then pull out because I don't want to come yet. I drag some of her moisture up to her asshole, spreading it around, and massaging her tight opening. She immediately moans and pushes back against me so I push a finger inside her and her breathing quickens and I know another orgasm is on the way for her.

I withdraw my finger, replacing it with my cock,

and pop the head inside her ass. She squeals at first, unused to the stretch, and after a moment pushes back into me, accepting more of my hard dick in her cute little bum. Pretty soon I'm fully seated inside her, riding her with one knee on either side of her hips. I lower myself onto her back and wrap my arms around her, turning her head to I can kiss the side of her face while I'm pounding her. She screams and begs for me to fuck her harder and I do until I can't anymore, and empty my load in her ass.

I realize my brothers have joined us on the floor for a better view and when I finally pull out and flip her to her back so I can see her pretty face, Niko has brought her a warm washcloth. He begins to clean her, scooping her languid body into his arms, and I hear her murmuring something.

"What is it, darlin'? What did you say?"

She opens her eyes fully. "I love you. I said I love you. Each of you. All of you."

A smile grows across Niko's face, which doesn't surprise me because he was the first of the three of us to fall in love with Charleigh.

"I love you too, baby," Kir says, bending to kiss her forehead.

I didn't think I'd ever see the day when he could find love with another woman after losing his Clara, and I'm happy for him, really happy.

As for me, I don't say anything, and Charleigh smiles at me anyway. I don't have to say it, because she knows what I'm thinking and feeling, and all the words in the world can't make life any sweeter than it is at this very moment.

CHAPTER THIRTY-FOUR

Charleigh

I'm not sure I've ever seen my little sister quite as excited as she is right now.

She's practically jumping out of her skin, checking the front door every few minutes while waiting for her friends to arrive for the Alekseev's big party.

Not that the guys ever would have said no anyway, but it was their idea to have Evie invite some of her friends. They wisely realized the only way she will ever be comfortable here, as part of their world, is if she can keep up her friendships. Her friends will have questions, she knows, but we practiced how to answer them, explaining this is where she lives now that her father is gone, and I'm her guardian.

After much pacing, she squeals and flings open the door, running out front, where I follow to watch her throw her arms around her friends. They jump up and down and scream like typical teenaged girls, and I'm both happy and sad at how normal it all seems.

I'm happy that my sister is so tickled, but also sad her joy is so contrived. She doesn't have the normal life of a teenager, where they learn the ways of the world under the watchful eye of parents, doing minor silly and stupid things that carry no great consequence other than learning a lesson or two that gets chalked up to 'life experience.'

That was never in the cards for her, just like it wasn't for me. When you have to raise yourself and your sibling, there's very little about life that is carefree.

Because of that, the lack of normalcy in her life, this new, unexpected chapter might be a step-up, although an unconventional one, to a different sort of happy life.

Beggars can't be choosers, yo.

When the girls arrive, they shower Evie with a barrage of nosy questions, which she handles like a champ. I hover in the background in case she needs me to run interference, but she diverts the attention from herself to the house and compound. Loaded with Cokes in their hands, Evie proudly shows them around, starting with her bedroom. This is where I let them do their thing, oohing and aahing over Evie's nice, new digs. I want to think she's not showing off or bragging, but I let it go. She's got to learn to use good judgement, and no amount of my hovering is going to help that develop.

Hell, she's going to be seventeen soon.

"Mmmm, that looks good," I say.

One of the gazillion security guards finishes stuffing a mini-sandwich in his mouth that he swiped from a catering tray. He blushes when I catch him and gulps it down so fast I don't know how he didn't choke.

"Oh, um, Miss Gates—"

I laugh and make him a plate of the small sandwiches. We have so much, anyway, and if we don't feed our employees, what the hell are we doing feeding guests?

"Take this back to the guard house so everyone can have some. And really, help yourself anytime," I say, pressing the plate into his hands.

He glances in the direction of the housekeeper, who I see scowling at him, and I make a mental note to talk to her later. In the past, it might not have been typical to share the catered food with security or other members of the team, but since I'm basically the 'lady of the house' now, I make these decisions.

Lady of the house. What a stupid, old-fashioned term. I need to come up with something better. I mean hell, I freaking *shot* a man. Actually, I shot two men, and killed one of them. I'm so much more than any *lady of the house.*

The guests begin to arrive, a carefully curated list of club members and others from outside the club. In spite of 'obligations' and crap like that, I convinced the guys to omit any of our 'difficult' members like the pervy old Alexei, and include only those we knew would be sure to appreciate a nice party, and who are capable of behaving.

There will be one guest I'm not too pleased about—the *Pakhan*—but the guys insisted there's no way around inviting him. Even if he never shows up, he still has to be on every invitation list, they tell me.

Oh, and I nearly forgot Dominika. Since I'm not at the club much these days—security concerns, and all—she's pretty much fallen off my radar. But her strange collection of photos still gnaws at me, and I don't get why the guys let it go so easily.

Something about 'picking battles,' they said, and insisted she be included.

But seriously, someone scratching your mother's

face out of a bunch of family photos? If it were my mom, I sure wouldn't let it go as easily.

Which reminds me. We made a final trip to my father's apartment before the landlord came to clear it out, and I found a box of photos albums in the back corner of a closet he must have forgotten. It looked like it hadn't been touched in the ten years since Mother has been gone. I only peeked at it, intending to bring it home to the compound and take my time going through it later.

What a treasure it turned out to be. There were photos of my parents before they were married, looking so happy and carefree when every possibility in the world was ahead of them, and there was nothing they thought they couldn't do. But life has a way of wearing on people, and the stresses of having children and a barely-surviving pawn shop didn't take long to show in their expressions, replacing the happy fullness of their younger faces.

Especially for my mother, her face became a map of the hardships of life with my father. She was still pretty, of course, but the light in her eyes was somewhat dimmed, her complexion dry and sallow. The worry lines between her eyebrows were, by that time, permanently etched.

I opened an album, the last one she must have filled before she died—my father had no interest in documenting our lives either before or after Mother passed—and in it were photos of a small birthday cake with ten candles. I'm smiling behind the little flames, no doubt on the edge of my seat waiting to blow them out, and I am happy the way a ten-year-old is with few cares in the world beyond who's coming to my slumber party. I looked at the date and realized it was only two days before my mother was murdered. That's a knife to the heart, and the pain that I thought was mostly gone reared its head again, an unkind reminder that I'll never be okay about losing my mother as a ten-year-old.

The guys were calling me to come down for dinner, so I stuffed everything back in the box, unsure of the right time to share it with Evie, when something slipped out of the back of an album.

Happy 10th birthday to my sweet Charleigh, the outside of the envelope said.

She forgot to give me my birthday card.

I flipped it over between my fingers for a minute, debating whether to open the seal on it and figured, why the hell not. The card was intended for me and even though ten years have passed, I have it now. I carefully break the glue on the seal and unfold the card to see the inside message.

My beautiful girl, know that I will always be with you. Love, Mom.

Well, that did it. I looked around my bedroom like someone had planted this thing or was playing a mean trick on me. But I know it's from Mother thanks to her unforgettable handwriting and the cheap Dollar Store cards she always chose.

That card was sitting in that box for ten years, waiting for me. What are the chances? If I hadn't found those things, they would have gone to the dump with Pops's other things, and probably incinerated as if they never existed.

As if my mother and I never existed.

How I want her back. I'd be happy for five minutes, just enough to feel her, smell her, and hear her words in my ears. Is that so much to ask for? I've never needed her more than I do now. I need her to help me navigate raising an ornery teenager, the love of three strong men, and a new life where I carry a weapon, since I never know when I'll need to defend myself.

But as luck would have it, all I get is this card, and maybe that's enough to be thankful for, a reminder that Mother is here with me all the time, even when I don't know it, and that if she weren't, things might be much, much more strange than they already are.

CHAPTER THIRTY-FIVE

Charleigh

The party was held mostly under a huge white canopy in the backyard with music playing, drinks flowing, and lots of good, catered food. I, for one, ate way too much sushi, never a good idea at a party because you might end up with fish breath.

Which wasn't a problem, Evie assured me, after she was kind enough to let me breathe on her.

Sisters.

During the party, I hung back for a time, watching not only my sister but also the guys. It's funny how they're brothers when they are also so different. Now that I know them, like really know them, I see things I never would have noticed a few weeks ago.

Vadik is pressing the flesh with the guests who

come through the door, but also keeping an eye on the big picture, making sure everyone has a drink and that hors d'oeuvres are passed generously. Kir is surrounded by people laughing at his jokes who are also sucking down beers, slapping each other on the back, and making all kinds of noise. Then there's Niko, whose beauty is admired by every woman he passes as well as some men, engaging in quiet one-on-one conversations where he makes every person he spends time with feel like they're the only person in the room.

They complement each other, these guys really do.

I have a better time than I even hoped, and the guys seem happy with how things go, as well. Dominika, to her credit, steers clear of me.

With the party eventually winding down, Evie's little friends leave, and I put her to work throwing out empties and making sure glassware is returned to the kitchen. She's in such a good mood she doesn't protest, not even for a moment, and I work alongside her until Vadik walks up to us.

"You know, you don't have to do this. We have staff who do this work," he says.

Evie sets down what she's doing, eager to be let off the hook.

Not a chance.

"Thanks, Vadik, we realize that, but it's important we pitch in. I want to make sure Evie remembers not all teenagers live in mansions surrounded by household help."

Evie clicks her tongue loudly and I catch her rolling her eyes like she does dozens of times a day. But she gets back to work, although not without her usual litany of long, loud, dramatic sighs.

Vadik makes himself scarce before he laughs out loud.

"Evie," I say when we've made a good dent in the after-party mess, "let's take a little walk."

The compound is big enough to feel like you're away and off the property, even when you aren't, which is a godsend.

"So how are things going for you here?" I ask her.

She shrugs. "It's nice. My friends all liked it."

Of course. I think back to the days when what my friends thought was the most important thing in the world. Glad those days are past. They were torturous.

She nudges me, giggling. "They also think your boyfriends are hot."

Hmmm. My *boyfriends*. I hadn't thought of them like that. These guys are a lot of things to me, but boyfriend is one term I hadn't thought to use.

"Glad they think so," I say, hoping to end the conversation.

Evie pulls her phone out of her pocket, and I hear it vibrating lightly. "Oh, Char, do you mind if I go back to the house? Everyone's posting their photos of the party now and I want to be the first to see them."

"Yeah, sure."

I find the old hammock, the one that the guys told me their father used to love, and crawl into it, warmed by the dappled light sneaking through the tree canopy. I wonder what it was like to be Grigory Alekseev, Russian immigrant who made it big the only way he knew how, who later perished with his beloved wife in a raging house fire.

Bizarre how both my and the Alekseevs' parents died under terrible circumstances. I've often wondered if in some way it's more than just a coincidence, to have this in common with the guys. But I push that out of my mind. I'm drowsy in the sun and want to close my eyes for just a bit to see if I can make up for the lack of sleep I've been getting a night.

Just a few minutes of napping would be so nice…

CHAPTER THIRTY-SIX

Charleigh

I'm in that in-between place where you know you're not asleep yet, but you know you almost are.

Is there a name for that?

Anyway, I turn over on my side to wait for my momentary nap time to arrive, when a shadow blocks the sun's rays from my face, and I actually become chilly.

When the sun doesn't come back out, and I can't doze because I'm no longer warm, I open one eye to see if afternoon clouds have blown in and whether it looks like rain.

I push myself up and take a deep breath to start screaming.

Because Dimitri is standing right over me.

Before I can get a sound out, or really even move,

his hand covers my mouth and pushes me right back into the hammock, leaving me with no leverage for doing anything other than kicking my feet.

Which I do until he sits on my legs.

"Pretty girl," he coos at me, "I've been waiting for this moment."

God no. Just no. How did he...

I try to remain calm. His open palm is covering my mouth and almost my nose. He could suffocate me if he wanted to.

"Tsk, tsk, tsk. You had a party and didn't invite me? That's very rude, you know."

He's evil. Pure evil.

His gaze travels from my face to my polka-dotted sundress, now straining across my breasts because of the position I'm in. He runs a finger from his free hand over them, and then takes a handful and kneads my flesh hard, until it hurts.

I try to scream from behind his hand, but nothing comes out besides muffled groans.

"Huh," he says, looking at me with curiosity. "I thought you were the type to like it rough. After all, I've seen the video of the guys giving it to you in the ass."

Huh?

My stomach roils. I'm sinking. Sinking into the terror that's danced around me these recent weeks.

It's hammering me without mercy, pulling me into the abyss like a lead weight. I squeeze my eyes shut like that will make it go away. It doesn't.

Mother, where are you? I need you.

He laughs quietly. "Yup, that's right, I have cameras in the assholes' house. Well, just the library but, boy, has that paid off. Fuck me, baby, you are hot. If only they'd had that goddamn auction, I could have brought you home and made you into a real woman. Taught you the pleasures of the flesh in a way the fucking Alekseev brothers can't even dream of. But it is what it is. I'll take what I can get, even if it is sloppy seconds."

I force my eyes to open in the hope that I can connect with whatever sliver of humanity the man might have, but his eyes are dark, his pupils dilated with the excitement of finally getting what he's wanted all along.

I listen carefully to see if anyone's come to look for me or even if security is simply making their rounds. I hear nothing except the wind in the trees, and of course, Dimitri's disgusting words.

"Don't be scared, little girl. I'm not here to hurt you, at least not very much." He giggles.

I nod as best I can, even though he's holding me down, to try to communicate in some way with him. To remind him I'm a living, breathing human, rather than just a pawn in a long-standing fight with his rivals.

He smirks. "Oh, you're all nice and accommodating *now,* are you? After all the times you were such a rude bitch to me, acting like you were too good for me?"

I shake my head *no.*

"Whatever, Charleigh. All the women who get wrapped up with the Alekseevs think their shit doesn't stink. I mean, look at your club manager, Dominika. She's a bitch of epic proportion, all because of the years she spent fucking Grigory Alekseev. You know, the man who stole my share of the club?"

He releases my legs long enough to grab the hem of my dress and pull it up to my waist, and I think my God, it's finally happening. My biggest fear—that Dimitri would find me and make me do something I don't want to, marking me in some way he feels will ruin me for the Alekseevs.

"Hey, I like how your stomach healed. Looks really good." He tilts his head to study my jagged scars. "*Apology accepted.* Great way to send a message. I mean, you'll never forget me now, will you?"

I shake my head again.

Remain calm. Panic will just make it impossible to think.

He looks around like he's surprised no one's come looking for me yet. I'm surprised too.

"Look, I'm gonna remove my hand from your mouth but if you make even a little noise, I will take you out with a closed fist so hard you'll be out for hours and will be healing from a broken nose for weeks. I'm sure a pretty girl like you doesn't want that."

He slowly takes his hand away, and I move my bruised lips without a sound. I have to get him to trust me. Then I can make my move.

"Get up," he growls, grabbing the hair on the back of my head.

I manage to get my feet over the edge of the hammock and clumsily stand while being led by my hair. He begins to pull me to the edge of the property and I start to think this is it, he's either going to take me away, or kill me, or both.

This is how it ends. Just as I thought it might.

CHAPTER THIRTY-SEVEN

CHARLEIGH

Dimitri pulls me behind a hedge, dragging me by the hair until I'm dizzy from the motion. I cough and heave, but nothing comes up, as if my body won't even give me that little bit of relief.

"Stop that," he snarls, slapping my face with his free hand.

The sting surprises me, and I look at him. "Please, please, Dimitri," I say softly, "let me go. Leave while you can. You know the guys will find you regardless of what you do to me."

He considers my words. "Yes, I suppose they will find me someday. I've accepted that. But not until I take away the one thing that is most important to them."

Tears seep from the corners of my eyes, and all I

can think is to hope the guys will take care of Evie. I know she's difficult, but there is no one to look after her besides me. I want her to have better than I had. She has so much ahead of her.

Dimitri pushes me down in a muddy spot under the bushes, pinning me while he opens his pants. I lie there, trying to think clearly enough to remember some of what I learned in my self-defense classes. If I can get him in a vulnerable position…

I hold still, as if I'm resigned to what's coming, waiting for my chance to do something, anything to get away from this human scum. When he releases my arms to pull down my panties, I close my fist and swing as hard as I can against his temple.

While this kills my hand, I know it won't cause *him* enough pain for me to get away. It does, however, surprise him enough to stop what he's doing for a second. I squirm out of his hold, scrambling away, but he catches one of my feet and pulls me back.

Dammit.

"Ha-ha," he says. "Thought you could pull one over on me, huh? Well, now you're gonna pay. I will have you, and then leave you for dead. They won't find you for days, not until well after the local coyotes make a meal of you."

A wave of anger fills me. This is *not* the end. No. Fucking. Way.

This will not be how I go out.

He crawls over me until he's sitting on my chest, pinning my arms, and begins to aim his penis at my mouth. I open as if I'm going to take it, but at the last moment, with a burst of all the strength I have left, I free one arm and reach under him to twist his balls. I don't let go.

In a second, he is howling like an injured animal, and while his face is full of red fury, his hands instinctively fly to his crotch, releasing his hold on me. Now that he's weakened with pain, I give one more yank, push him aside, and finally get up to run.

"Help!" I scream. "Somebody, help me!"

I head for the house, without glancing back. He might be right on my tail or still doubled over in pain, but I'm not slowing enough to find out.

Three security guards appear, followed by the Niko, Kir, and Vadik. They are racing in my direction, looks of horror on their faces when they see my torn and dirty clothes. As soon as the first one reaches me, I fall to my knees, sobbing.

"There," I gasp, pointing, "in the bushes. By the hammock."

Niko stays with me while the guys run off, and I throw my arms around him. "Niko, Niko," I cry, barely able to speak between my sobs, "it was Dim... Dim..."

I can't finish.

He holds me by the shoulders. "Was it Dimitri, baby?"

I nod, falling onto all fours as my body is wracked with heaves.

I've got to pull it together. I can't let Evie see me like this.

I sniffle and when the nausea passes, let Niko help me to my feet. "Don't tell Evie, please don't tell Evie. Don't take me to the house. Take me to your cottage. She can't see me."

"All right, come on, baby," he says, scooping me into his arms and carrying me.

I throw my arms around his neck and bury my face in his chest, breathing his familiar scent, and I'm instantly comforted. We get to his cottage and he lays me on the sofa, leaving me, then returning with a warm washcloth.

He's dabbing at the dirt on my face when the rest of the guys join us.

I push myself up. "Did you get him? Did you get him?" I ask, pleading.

Please say yes.

But Kir shakes his head. "He got away. Fucker disabled the electricity in the fence."

I look at the security guys behind him. He had to have help. I know it.

Someone on the compound is helping Dimitri.

"This is such bullshit—" I start to say. "I was attacked *again,* and still you guys do nothing about it."

I push myself to my feet. "Go fuck yourselves. All of you."

They're lucky I don't twist *their* balls.

I head for the door.

Vadik raises his arm. "Hold on, Charleigh. We should have the attack on video. We'll take that to the *Pakhan—*"

But I cut him off. I am so over hearing about what the *Pakhan* wants. "The *Pakhan* can fuck himself, too. And I'll say that to his face. As far as I'm concerned, you can't keep me safe. None of you can, in spite of all your promises. So you might as well just stop pretending you can. Admit it. You can't keep me safe."

CHAPTER THIRTY-EIGHT

Charleigh

I tear off my clothes and stuff them into the bathroom trash, then stomp into a scalding hot shower. I know it's completely illogical, but I soap up a washcloth and scrub my skin until it's bright red and even then, I don't stop. I can't. Dimitri might not have gotten away with what he'd planned, but his touch has left me soiled in a way I'm not sure I'll ever be able to get rid of.

On top of feeling ugly and dirty, I am also so furious that at this moment in time, someone could look at me wrong and I'd kill them with my bare hands. Seriously. That's how enraged I am. Mad at everyone. Mad at the world.

I'm mad at my mother for leaving me when I was ten, and for my father for all his bad decisions. I'm mad at Evie that she can't just behave, stay on track like other teenagers, and not add to my worries.

I'm mad at the guys for messing up my life, for taking me from my father to auction me, then creating a situation where I can never leave them.

I've been failed over and over and all I know now is that I'm the only person I can rely on, no one will ever be there for me, no one ever has been, and I have to stop hoping otherwise.

While the hot water beats down on me, there's a knock on my bathroom door. My first impulse it to tell whoever it is to fuck off, but I figure it's Evie wanting to show me her photos from the party. When I holler *come in,* it's Kir's head that pokes around the corner.

Just what I need.

"Hey," I call over the shower noise.

Through the glass, I watch him approach, his gaze locked on mine. He kicks off his shoes and opens his jeans, letting them fall to the floor, along with the rest of his clothes until he's standing there stark naked and hot as fucking shit.

Oh damn. I am so not in the mood to be nice.

And yet.

He pulls the elastic at the back of his head and his hair tumbles to his shoulders. With his thick cock hanging heavy between his legs, he pulls open the shower door and joins me.

"Damn, this water's hot."

I watch the stream bounce off his hard muscles into little beads that become airborne before they fill the air with a thick, steamy mist. He fills his palm with shampoo, turns me to face away, and starts to massage it into my scalp.

Plain and simple, his fingers are like magic and I instantly turn to putty under them, his deep pressure releasing all manner of toxic thoughts until I have to hold onto the shower wall just to stay upright.

"Amazing, Kir, amazing," I mutter, not even caring whether he can hear me over the sound of the water.

But apparently, he can. "I used to do this for Clara," he says easily.

Holy shit. I've never heard him speak so casually about her.

He rinses the shampoo with my help and I turn to face him. "You've never really talked about her." I study his face, trying to see what's changed.

He nods, and then starts soaping my body, paying special attention to my breasts, of course. "Yeah. I know. But it feels good to. It makes me feel like she's… I don't know, watching over me or something." Embarrassed, he laughs and shrugs his shoulders.

At this point, his cock is hard and when I move closer to him, it presses against my stomach, sending tingles through my core. I haven't forgotten my traumatic experience of the day, but his touch is soothing. I fall into his arms, and we kiss for what seems like hours.

Eventually, I turn around, bending forward, and he enters me from behind like he can read my mind and he knows what I want and need, which I guess is at least partially true. He did after all, know to come get in the shower with me when I was at my pretty damn lowest.

He puts his hands on my shoulders for purchase as he pumps in and out of my hungry pussy, the water still beating down on us. His perfectly rhythmic fucking has put me into a trance, eyes closed, mouth slack, head bobbing reflexively every time he bottoms out and I think maybe life isn't so bad and that my mother is watching over me.

Although I wouldn't want her watching this.

CHAPTER THIRTY-NINE

Niko

I have an iron grip on Charleigh's arm, but I'm afraid even that won't keep her in her seat.

Anger, hate, resentment, and dishonesty are par for the course in my day-to-day life. They're just part of my world. There's no escaping it. In fact, on the days where I don't come across it, I actually notice it missing, that's how much it is the norm. I grew up around it, and now I live in it.

Not that anyone sees that on my face. I'm observant enough to keep my own expression neutral, something a lot of people around me could benefit from trying themselves. Papa used to say it was one of my best qualities, my quiet watchfulness. I'm not sure it's what I would have picked as a strength, given the choice, but I can't deny it's served me well.

I think there was a time when Charleigh could smile brightly, masking any real emotion she might be feeling. She was brought up to be polite that way, to never hurt anyone's feelings or offend anyone. She wanted to be *liked* and in doing so always made her own feelings secondary to others'.

But she sure as hell is not on board with doing that today. Her lips are drawn into a thin grimace, and even though the room is cool, with my clear view of her profile, I can see tiny droplets of perspiration wetting the wispy hairs on her temples. Her eyes are heavy-lidded to further emphasize the sneer she's wearing, which I am guessing is completely unconscious.

But the thing about her that gives her away the most, that really reveals how tightly wound she is, is her jittering leg, which hasn't stopped vibrating since we sat down.

I have no doubt that if she had a firearm on her, dead bodies would be littering the floor before our meeting with the *Pakhan* even gets underway.

"Thank you all for coming today," he says, looking around the room, which is divided in two like opposing teams.

On my side are my brothers, me, Charleigh, and a couple of our security guys.

On the other is Dimitri, wearing his usual maniacal grin, like he can't wait for the show to get started. If I didn't know better, I'd think he was an old friend who's happy to see me.

What I wouldn't do to get my hands around his neck right now.

With him are a couple motley-looking guys I don't know, probably part of his posse. Even though the man is as good as dead, he's still stupid enough to drag his lackeys around so that when he goes down, he won't be alone. He will expect them to defend him and in doing so, they will lose their lives too.

Not that I give a shit.

And overseeing this shitshow of a gathering is the *Pakhan,* arms on his massive desk, his fingers intertwined, almost as in prayer. His head slowly swivels as he takes in all his visitors, and as usual, his expression doesn't give away a damn thing except for when he offers Charleigh a polite nod, just like he would any woman.

Beside him but one step back is his second, that annoying fuck of a man. His chest is puffed out self-importantly, which almost makes me laugh out loud. It's those who are overly impressed with themselves who are the most fragile and easy to knock over. And I am pretty sure this man's delusions of grandeur are coming to a screeching halt soon. The

Pakhan does not suffer fools, and I have no doubt he can clearly see what's just before him.

He clears his throat. "I don't like this. I don't like what any of you are doing. It has to stop."

There's really no question about what he's referring to, but for clarification, Vadik speaks up. "I… we, my brothers and I, understand that. And we regret how that has negatively impacted the region."

We knew fucking up Dimitri's businesses would not go over well with the *Pakhan*. Not only has our blowing up his buildings attracted the attention of the authorities, but interfering with his shipments hit everyone's pocketbooks. It was a calculated move we made, one we felt was justified.

In time, everyone in the region will be whole again. We'll make sure of it. But sometimes money is not the most important thing.

"As of today," the *Pakhan* says, "this open warfare will *stop*."

I'm still gripping Charleigh to hold her in place, and her shaking legs starts to move faster, like a car with no brakes. Jesus, I've got to keep her under control. I understand the distress she's in, but she's got to keep it together, at least for now.

"I don't know, *Pakhan*," Dimitri says as if he's offended, "these Alekseevs have caused nothing but trouble since my father died—"

"And that's why you killed our parents, right?" Kir interrupts.

Dimitri slams his hand on the soft arm where he sits. "I've told you, I am not behind that. I did not do it. I did not kill your parents, nor did I kill Charleigh's father."

At the mention of her name, her head jerks in Dimitri's direction, which was probably his plan. He tilts his head and smiles at her.

I hold her arm even tighter.

The *Pakhan* raises his hands before bringing them back together. "I've always said things are often not as they seem. I say that to everyone. For example, *you*, yes you, step over there." He points a finger.

The *Pakhan*'s second is surprised he's being singled out, proud he's worthy of acknowledgement. He takes up position where the *Pakhan* is pointing and holds his hands together in front of him, lowering his chin to affect some false modesty.

"I've always said your pride, boy, will be the death of you, and today it will," the *Pakhan* says.

Confusion crosses the second's face and is quickly replaced with fear. "What? Sir? I'm sorry, but I don't know what you mean."

The *Pakhan* sighs impatiently. "I know what you've been up to. Every action you take is to further yourself. You care about nothing else, not even the brotherhood. I know the role you played in the murder of the Alekseevs. You were afraid your position, that of my right-hand-man, might go to one of the brothers if they weren't committed to running their father's businesses. With Grigory Alekseev out of the way, you knew none of the brothers could take this position, because they had to carry on their father's work."

The second's mouth flaps open, then closes, then opens again like a fish gasping for air. Before he can get it together and protest the condemnation, the *Pakhan* stands, holding a pistol. He takes aim, fires, and the huge man crumbles to the ground.

Charleigh screams and grabs me, burying her face in my chest. I gladly hold her.

But the second isn't gone yet. "You bastard," he yells weakly at the *Pakhan,* "I had nothing to do with the Alekseev's fire. Dominika did." His head drops back on the floor. He's losing blood too fast to say much more. In moments, the life will leave his body.

What? Dominika?

That just doesn't sound right. She was my father's mistress. He was good to her, or as good to her as he was to any mistress.

I pull Charleigh tighter. She doesn't need to see the blood splatter some poor slob will have to clean later.

"As for you," the *Pakhan* says, turning toward Dimitri, "you have bucked my instructions too many times. I let you slide again and again and again out of respect for your father, who was my friend. But I think that if your father were alive today, he'd agree with what I'm about to do."

Just as the *Pakhan* raises his pistol, Charleigh bolts out of my arms, and jumps in front of him.

"Charleigh, no!" Kir screams.

She holds her hands up in front of the *Pakhan*. "With all due respect, sir, you need to let me do this. You owe it to me. Everyone here owes it to me."

The *Pakhan* steps around Charleigh, but she gets in front of him again.

I want to tell her that what she's doing is a good way to die, but I can't speak. So I get up to pull her out of the way.

But before I reach her, the *Pakhan* looks at Vadik, who nods his approval. Charleigh takes the pistol.

The man is accommodating Charleigh. I never thought I'd see the day.

"You are correct, young lady," he says with a little bow. "You have earned the right to do this." He passes her the gun, which she takes with nothing but pure confidence.

Both pride and sadness wash through me at the same time. The scene before me proves that our girl can truly fend for herself now, but also that her innocence is gone. Permanently.

Dimitri's face is covered in panic. Can he really be surprised this is how he's going to meet his end? Did he really think the *Pakhan* was going to send him on his way after his scolding?

"Wait, Charleigh, wait," Dimitri pleads. "Can we please talk? Just for a minute? I have some things to tell you. Important things." His voice cracks. He really didn't see any of this coming.

How is that even possible?

Taking aim with absolutely no hesitation, doubt, or sorrow, Charleigh fires the *Pakhan's* gun like she has wanted to for so long. Her face shows no emotion and my fear is that she can kill all the Dimitris in the world and still not be satisfied.

The guys with him reach for their guns, but with one look around the room, they stop. At this point, any effort on their part would be futile. And deadly.

"Hey. He's trying to say something," one of them says, hovering over him.

I cross the room and the dying Dimitri waves me closer. There's something so incongruous about seeing a childhood friend dying in front of you, knowing he deserves it, but also remembering the days you freely played, without a care in the world.

It's heartbreaking, when it comes down to it. Tragic, even.

"Niko," Dimitri whispers, "Niko, I didn't do it. I swear. I didn't kill them, I didn't."

He's reaching, wanting a connection, a hand to hold onto in his last minutes, but I think of the carving on Charleigh's stomach and I can't comfort the man. I just can't.

"Do you know who did it, Dimitri? Now is the time to tell us," I urge.

"Dominika. Talk to Dominika," he rasps as he takes his last breath. "The second was in on it, but it was Dominika."

A punch to the gut doesn't begin to describe the hit I feel in my stomach. The light in Dimitri's eyes fades quickly as I absorb—as we all do, really—his news.

Charleigh chokes back a sob when she realizes Dimitri is gone, and I see my brothers are as slack-jawed as I am, in complete and utter shock at his accusation.

It can't be true. It just can't.

Dominika?

Dominika had something to do with my parents' murder?

"Well," the *Pakhan* says, patting Charleigh on the back, "what a stone-cold bitch we have on our hands here. Tell me, Miss Gates, do you plan on joining the brothers' team permanently? They could probably use someone like you."

He's wearing a reptilian smile, something I've only seen on him a handful of times.

She looks at him, expressionless, clearly not appreciating what he probably meant as a true compliment. "No. I am not going to work for them."

The *Pakhan*'s eyebrows rise and he scoffs.

"They are going to work for *me*," she says, throwing the three of us a coy wink.

She bursts out laughing, a sound I haven't heard from her in way too long, and everyone joins, even the *Pakhan*.

CHAPTER FORTY

Niko

I don't love, or even like, that my girl is unburdened by killing someone. It's not a good thing to get used to, this thirst for revenge. I've seen it rot many a man from the inside out, and it would slay me for the same to happen to Charleigh.

The four of us head for the door, when the *Pakhan* stops us. "Before you go, a minute more of your time please."

I want to get Charleigh out of there as quickly as possible, considering there are two dead bodies in the room. I position her where she can't see them and am tempted to tell the *Pakhan* to make it quick.

But I am more polite than that. "Sure, *Pakhan,* what's on your mind?" I ask.

He turns to Charleigh. "Remember, Miss Gates, when I said things are not always as they seem?"

Charleigh nods. "I do remember that."

Typical *Pakhan*, talking in riddles.

"I've known for some time about what Dimitri shared tonight," he says.

"What do you mean?" Charleigh asks.

He sits on the corner of his desk, the most casual thing I think I've ever seen him do. His generation of men are big on decorum. Papa never sat *on* his desk, either, only behind it in his chair.

He continues. "I've been doing some investigating of my own, or rather, my men have. We put a trail on Dimitri. One morning, several weeks ago, he went to the bank. Your club manager, Dominika, went in right after him. I thought this was very interesting," he says, holding up a finger.

He picks up the heavy crystal glass on his desk and takes a swig, of what, I have no idea. He offered us nothing when we arrived. This was not a social call. "I later confronted him, Dimitri. True to form, he spilled his story like a scared little girl. He was blackmailing Dominika and they were carrying out their transaction at the bank. *She* is the one who killed your parents. The second helped her for his own reasons."

"But—" Kir starts to say.

The *Pakhan* stops him by holding up his hand. "Wait. There's more."

Holy fucking shit.

"She did it in a jealous rage because your father rejected her appeals, one too many times, to become Mrs. Grigory Alekseev. It was her life goal to replace your mother, which comes as no surprise. She wanted to be part of a family. She was tired of the sidelines, watching, being left out. So, she killed them both, knowing Dimitri would be blamed, and when he figured out it was her, he made her pay him for his trouble. Then, she shot Miss Gates's father, knowing everyone would think Dimitri did it again. If you guys went after him and got rid of him, he couldn't bribe her anymore. Problem solved."

Dominika, my God. She killed the man she supposedly loved? A scorned woman… and all that.

Vadik rubs his head. "She must have stolen the money from the club to pay him. That's why we were short."

The *Pakhan* turns to Charleigh again. "So you see, Miss Gates, you thought I was doing nothing, when in fact, I was doing everything. But, no need to thank me. Watching the Alekseev boys try to handle you will be payment enough." He shakes with laughter at his joke.

Charleigh laughs along with him although I'm

not sure she thinks he's as funny as he does. "Is Dominika at the club right now?" she asks.

"Oh, that," the *Pakhan* says with a smile, "I almost forgot. No, she's not at the club. She won't be coming to work today. Or tomorrow. Or the day after."

CHAPTER FORTY-ONE

Charleigh

Dimitri is dead. Dominika is dead.

The words replay in my head.

"Fuck all," Vadik says. "Under our noses the whole time, she was. We trusted her. She joined our family for holidays and graduations. And she fucking killed our parents." He looks down at his glass of scotch, shaking his head in disbelief.

The news about their parents has understandably sent the guys into a funk, probably along the lines of what they went through when they first lost them. I've been there, myself. Just when I start to think I'm over losing my mother, the grief comes roaring back and bites me in the ass, often when I least expect it.

It's a funny thing to have in common, that both the Alekseevs and I lost our parents to murder. It's like we're in this small, special club, the kind of club no one ever wants to join. The circumstances might be different, but what they have in common is that these people were taken before their time, taken from us by evil people. I might have been a child when it happened to me, and the Alekseevs are adults, but it leaves you bereft, nonetheless. The loss is a huge, gaping maw, threatening to eat you alive unless you find a way to fight it.

To think that when I found those weird photos, where Mrs. Alekseev's face had been scratched out, the guys actually gave Dominika a pass. They brushed it off as no big deal, just another odd thing about a quirky person.

"Hey, do you think she swiped those photos when the fire was set? The ones where she scratched your mother's face out?" I ask.

Kir runs his fingers through his hair. "She must have. Shit, that was a big fucking clue we missed. Shows how loyalty to someone can blind you to something right in front of your face. If we'd looked more closely, we might have realized those photos came from the house, not Dominika's own personal stash."

Bet they'll never let that happen again. But on the other hand, is there *anyone* these guys can trust? They've been betrayed left and right, and while they've avenged the wrongs done against them, the betrayal must still sting.

"You know, you think danger comes from the outside, but that's such a limited view. I mean, it never even crossed my mind that Dominika did it, killed Mama and Papa. Which I guess is what she wanted. She knew Dimitri would have to take the heat, no matter how much he denied it," Niko says.

Personally, I think they should have suspected Dominika from the start. I know they didn't see the side of her that I did, how cruelly she treated other people, but they knew she wasn't a nice lady. That much was obvious.

I keep that thought to myself, though, and also don't mention when they didn't believe me about Dominika setting Stacey up to be hurt by Alexei. The guys are already beating themselves up, anyway.

Kir looks my way. "You know, Charleigh, I'm proud of you. We all are."

I raise an eyebrow at him. "What do you mean?"

"You've faced some difficult situations, and you handled them. You're strong. I know your life hasn't been easy these last weeks," he says.

Niko smooths his hands over his thighs. "And that's why we don't want to let you go."

"That's not the only reason," Kir adds.

"True. But… we wanted to talk about the future," Niko says.

For once, I feel like I'm ready for this conversation.

Or not.

I look at Vadik, who's stoic as usual, which I suppose is one of the things that tickles me about him most. He's like a pineapple on the outside—rough and prickly—but juicy and sweet on the inside. Most people never get past his badass exterior. I am one of the lucky few. And I love it.

I love *him*.

I love all three of these men. We've flourished together under the strangest of circumstances and come out on top. We've overcome betrayal, threats on our lives, and massive loss. And it has, somehow, brought us closer.

I know that if I stick with these guys, I'll never really be completely safe, as good as it feels to know Dimitri will not be coming after me again. His death is a massive relief but there's no guarantee another Dimitri won't come along at some point. If that happens, we'll deal with it.

But I'm feeling pretty fucking safe right now. And I'm not going anywhere. Although I would like to get back into my classes.

"What about Evie?" I ask.

I'm sure I don't have to tell them Evie and I are a two-for-one package deal. They take the two of us, or nothing. It's that simple.

Vadik leans back in his chair. "How do you think she'd like boarding school? There are excellent places we could send her, and she'd be around other kids, have the chance to start over."

Boarding school? Evie?

I want to laugh at the idea, but the more I think about it, the more I think she just might go along with it. "We'll ask her. See what she thinks. But what about security?"

"Some of these schools, the children of royalty attend. Their security has to be top notch," Vadik says.

Wow. Just wow. For one of the first times in my life, I am breathing easily. Not to say life will never throw me another curve ball—I'm not that lucky—but I feel like I can handle what comes my way with the support of the guys.

My phone vibrates with a call from an unknown number. I usually ignore those, but something is telling me to answer this one.

"Hello?"

There's a gasp on the other end of the line. "Oh thank God you answered, Charleigh. I wasn't sure you would."

"Victoria?"

"Yes, honey, it's me," she says, her voice cracking. "How are you?"

Good question, I'm just trying to figure out that myself.

"Things are good, Vic. Better than they've been in a long time. Pops is gone, but I think you know that."

She sniffles. "I do. And I'm so sorry. I wanted to be in touch sooner, but I wasn't sure it was safe."

"You're safe, Vic. You have nothing to worry about. In fact, why don't you come over to the Alekseev's house? It would be great to see you."

"No. No, I can't do that, Charleigh. I'm not safe. I never will be."

"Why? What kind of danger are you in?" I ask.

The guys look up from their conversation and start to listen.

"I've never been safe, and I never will be, Charleigh. Please understand, I have something to tell you I've been hiding for years. Now that your father and the shop are gone, I feel like you should know."

I give a little laugh at her dramatics. "What, Vic? What could be so bad?"

"Charleigh. I was there when your mother was murdered."

CHAPTER 42

Charleigh

A kick straight to my gut couldn't have hit me harder.

"Wh… what do you mean?" I ask, stumbling to a chair.

Niko mouths *is everything all right?,* but I raise a finger to ask him to give me a minute.

"Y… you were there? When Mother was killed? How? Why?" I ask, my mouth going dry.

Thank goodness I'm sitting because the room is beginning to move around me, and I think I may be sick.

"I was there. So was your sister, Evie."

"What?" I ask in a whisper.

"I don't think Evie remembers anything. In fact,

I'm sure she doesn't, Char. I don't know that I'd tell her, at least not until she gets older."

The guys are gathered around me now, listening only to my half of the conversation but having no trouble picking up what we're talking about.

"Your mom was working in the shop, and Evie and I had just come in the back door after getting ice cream. We heard loud voices, so we hid, which was easy to do. You know all the junk your father kept there."

Not Evie. Please, not Evie.

"They kept yelling at your mom, something about money. I thought it was a simple hold up and that they'd eventually leave after she gave them what they wanted. But when I listened more carefully, they were talking about getting the money your father owed them. Charleigh, they killed your mom as a message to your dad. He owed these men money. I don't know what for, just that it must have been a lot."

The shaking starts in my hands, and I struggle to hold the phone to my ear, so I switch to hands free and place it on the coffee table before me. Then, the trembling moves up my body and my teeth chatter even though I'm not cold. I'm pretty sure I'm going to be sick, and I don't care if I barf all over the Alekseev house.

Pops was responsible for Mother's death?

Pops? My father? Mother's husband? He fucked her over just like he did me, just like the guys suspected.

"I'm sorry, Charleigh, sweetie. I'm so sorry, I wanted to tell you before, so many times, but I just couldn't. Your dad was all you girls had left and I didn't want you to hate him, at least not while you were young."

So now I can hate him, now that he's dead? Can you hate a dead person?

All these years he told us it was a random hold up. Just some guy with a gun, looking for quick and easy cash. Pawn shops get held up all the time, Pops told me. Rotten luck, he insisted.

Fucking liar. I swear, if he weren't already dead, I might be tempted to put a gun to his head.

My own father.

"I… I can't believe it, Vic," I say in a small voice. "My dad. His debts killed my mother. And yet he still didn't stop."

Why? Oh, why?

How could he do this to us? He ruined our family. For something that was avoidable.

"I know this is hard, honey," Victoria says. "In time, you'll be able to put it behind you like I did. Your mother was my friend. It wasn't easy for me to forgive your father, but I did. Your mother would have wanted it."

Mother. What would she say if she were here?

I'll never know.

I'll never see her, hear her voice, feel her touch.

I start spiraling into despair. But I stop myself. I'm not going there, goddammit. I refuse. I'm still here. I have a life to live. That's one thing my parents gave me, a life to live, and I'm going to live it.

"So why can't we see you, Vic?" I ask.

"Honey, I've been looking over my shoulder since the day your mother was murdered, and I will continue to as long as I'm on this earth. I saw the killers. Now that your dad and the shop are gone, I'm out of here. You will never see me again, but I will try to call from time to time."

"No, Vic—"

"Don't look for me, Charleigh. It will only bring us both trouble. My rent is paid until the end of the month. Behind a false wall in my closet is your mother's wedding dress and some other things. Go get them before the landlord cleans the place out. Remember I love you and your sister. Please take care of yourselves."

And she's gone.

I double over in tears, and when they finally taper off, I look up to find the guys circling me, like they always will, like they've promised, and while I know life will always throw no end of curve balls, they will be easier to accept with these men at my side.

EPILOGUE...

Two years later...

Evie waves at the four of us from her high school auditorium stage, where she's accepting her diploma. She still has more black shit around her eyes than I prefer, and now has a septum piercing, but boarding school got her on track with straight A's, so I really have nothing to complain about.

The headmaster, or principal, or whatever they call people in these fancy places, stops what he's doing and gives her a quick hug. He knows she's been through some shit, and has been her biggest supporter and fan.

After me, of course.

And the guys.

I grab Niko's hand because he's sitting next to me, and squeeze it. I could be wrong, but I'm pretty sure he's tearing up.

Of course, I am too. There have been so many milestones lately.

Like my own graduation. I downplayed it so it didn't overshadow Evie's. I finished my bookkeeping certificate and stuck around the local city college to earn my two-year degree. While Evie will go all the way with her education, my little diploma is the first anyone in my family has ever earned. My mother would be so proud.

I suppose my father would, too.

There was no funeral for Pops, no 'celebration of life,' nor any sort of remembrance. The guys took care of his cremation but I don't know where they stored his ashes. I asked that they not be buried with my mother. After I learned the real story behind her death, it didn't seem right to leave them together for eternity.

The twelve-year anniversary of my mother's death just passed, and I acknowledged it by putting flowers on her grave. We got her a proper headstone, something my father never bothered with, and we're now paying to have her gravesite regularly maintained. It felt good to visit and have a conversation with her in my head. I've stopped all my 'why' questions, where for years I didn't understand what happened. I still don't and have accepted I never will.

Sometimes there are no answers to questions. The 'why,' the wondering, and the questioning, have to be left behind. I carried them around long enough, and now that

I've shed their weight—or at least most of it—I am a different person.

Actually, a lot of things have conspired to make me a different person. I don't feel good about all of them.

For example, I don't feel good about killing Dimitri Yegorov. I don't regret it, but I also don't feel good about it. It was a necessary evil, if I ever wanted to live in peace. Now that time has passed, I find I have compassion for him, as miserable and tortured as he must have been. It's better for all of us that he's gone, don't get me wrong, it's just too bad he couldn't save himself from himself.

Same goes for Dominika. She was as evil as they come, that wretched woman, and is another person better off dead. She caused so much pain and destruction and while we never have gotten definitive proof, we think she was the one behind the car crash that killed Clara, as well as the one that killed Stacey. The Pakhan never divulged what he did with her, but I have no doubt she's dead, her body or ashes dumped somewhere in an unceremonious fashion. That's all she deserved.

The one downside to the Pakhan taking the lead on getting rid of her is that none of us got to have a final conversation with her. But what would we have said? What would we have asked?

More questions to which there are likely no answers, or at least none of the answers we want.

I finger my mother's locket while the new graduates

stream out of the auditorium, each heading to their families for photo time. Evie bounds up to us and Kir hands her a huge bouquet of her favorite flowers.

The same kind our mother loved so much.

Now that Evie is eighteen, an adult, and off to college, I know I have to tell her the story of what happened with our mother. It seems cruel to share something so devastating when everything in her life is looking so positive, but if I don't tell her soon, I know I'll chicken out and never do it.

Which might not be such a bad idea.

The guys have convinced me that honesty is the best policy, and even when important information is not happy news, it still needs to be shared.

But we won't tell her today. That's not the kind of graduation gift I'd wish on my worst enemy.

Still, it's going to be a hard conversation and I imagine my sister will go through the whole gamut of emotions I did two years ago, when I found out from Victoria.

Who, by the way, we have not heard a word from. It kills me, knowing nothing, but I have to believe she's doing what she needs to. When thoughts of how she is and whether anything has happened to her start swirling around my head, I remind myself, again, that we don't always get answers to our questions.

As frustrating as that is, it feels like my new mantra.

But one thing I am sure of, sure enough to bet my life

on, is that I have the full love and support of Vadik, Kir, and Niko.

The strong, sexy, devastatingly handsome Alekseev brothers.

"Are you ready?" Vadik asks Evie.

She looks over her shoulder at her friends, who are also tearing off their caps and gowns. She thrusts hers into my arms and plants a kiss on the cheek of each of the guys, saving a rib-cracking hug for me before she looks at me one more time and runs for the bus her other classmates are boarding, which will take them directly to the airport.

Lucky kids, they're on a graduation trip to London and Paris, where they are supposed to 'enrich their knowledge of art and history,' but where I imagine they'll basically goof off and consume all the wine and beer they can't here in the US.

But I'm not worried. Later tonight, the guys and I will board our own private jet and follow the kids so we can keep somewhat of an eye on them. We're not formal 'chaperones,' but we were desperate for a getaway and figured we could watch over Evie at the same time.

I swallow away the lump in my throat as Evie turns to wave at us one more time before climbing aboard the bus full of noisy teenagers.

Kir slings an arm around my shoulder. "Well then.

The kiddo is gone. Time for some adult fun. What do you say, baby?"

I look at my three guys and then at my watch. "We have a couple hours to pack, then we gotta get to the airport. I say we wait until the plane."

The guys laugh. "Our girl wants to join the mile high club," Vadik teases.

"What? Are you saying you guys are already members?" I ask.

They look at each other, no one saying a word.

"I knew it!" I laugh.

Cripes, is there anything these guys haven't done? I mean, can't I be their first for anything?

With one last wave at the bus, we head for the limo to take us home, and later to the airport.

Oh, what the hell.

I'll give the guys a taste of what's to come.

I raise the window separating us from the limo driver, and get on my knees in front of Kir. I lift my skirt up to bare my ass, unencumbered by panties, as per the guys' wishes.

The only time I wear panties anymore is when I willfully go against their demands because I am craving the spanking they promise to punish me with. I don't do it often, but when I do, it's fucking hot as hell.

I focus on opening Kir's trousers while Vadik or Niko —I'm not sure which—places his hands on my ass cheeks.

I shiver in anticipation of what, I don't yet know. But it will be something wild and orgasmic and memorable, just like the lives we're building together.

Do you love mafia romance?
Check out my next series, Dirty Mafia Games.

What happens next with Charleigh and her men?
Check out this BONUS Extended Epilogue
(https://dl.bookfunnel.com/iz4zg8oxjf)

EXTENDED EPILOGUE
Mika Lane

ABOUT THE AUTHOR

Dear Reader:

I'm USA TODAY bestselling romance author Mika Lane, and am OBSESSED with bringing you sassy, steamy stories with imperfect heroines and the bad-a*s dudes they bring to their knees. I'll always bring you my signature humor and heat, topped off with a modern-day happily ever after.

My first book ever was *The Day I Ate the Milkyway,* a true fourth-grade masterpiece illustrated with crayons and bound with construction paper and glue. Nowadays, steamy romance gives purpose to my days and nights as I create worlds and characters that tickle the imagination. I live in magical Northern California with my own handsome alpha dude, sometimes known as Mr. Mika Lane, and two devilish cats named Chuck and Murray.

A dual citizen of the United States and Ireland, I have on more than one occasion spent my last dollar on a plane ticket somewhere, and am always planning my next escape. I often try new recipes on unsuspecting friends, search out hiding places to read undisturbed, and sadly kill every houseplant I bring home.

I LOVE to hear from readers when I'm not dreaming up naughty tales to share. Visit my online shop https://mikalaneshop.com/ and say hello https://mikalaneshop.com/pages/meet-mika.

xoxo, Mika